Spanish Journals

The Posthumous Diary of an Expat

A R Lowe

A R Lowe ©2012

The right of A R Lowe to be identified as the author of this work has been asserted by him in accordance with the Copyright, Design and Patents Act 1988.

ISBN-13: 978-1481142441
ISBN-10: 1481142445

Introduction by Pamela Postlethwaite

This diary, written by my late husband, Ernest Postlethwaite, has been published expressly against his wishes, but with the full and hearty endorsement of my family and friends.

He did originally intend the diary, or 'journal', as he preferred to call it, to be published. Being a man of fixed ideas but very changeable temperament, I have interpreted his final utterance, "that blessed diary," as I have deemed most appropriate. The fact that these words were his last, apart from incoherent ramblings regarding documents, goats and relatives, indicates that his sole written work was foremost in his mind until the very end. It also suggests that he may have had a last minute change of heart regarding publication; 'blessed', after all, has more positive than negative connotations.

One rather clever family friend considers the diary, or journal, to be a historical document of the highest importance. "An anthropological delight," I recall him saying. He read it four times and told me that each reading brought more tears to the eye than the last. He suggested subtitling the work, *A Study of the Cross-Cultural Aspirations of a Middle-Class Englishman in the Early Twenty-first Century*, but I thought it rather long-winded and eventually chose a more fitting subtitle myself.

I leave you with this unadulterated transcript* of the first six months of the diary that Ernest kept diligently from November 2007 and hope that you are moved by it as much as we all were.

Pamela Postlethwaite,
Javea,
Spain
December 2012

* Including all his additional annotations (in parenthesis).

PART ONE - INTEGRATION

Thursday 1ˢᵗ November 2007

I am writing my first journal entry from the terrace of my house in Puebla de Don Arsenio, Alicante, Spain. A solemn moment! Today, I have read on the internet, is 'The Day of the Dead' here in Spain, but I myself feel very much alive, having at last cast off the shackles of the commuter's life. A life, it must be said, that has put me in the enviable financial position of enabling us to sell up and start a new life here at the relatively young ages of 54 (me) and 52 (Pamela). Pamela's mother dying so suddenly cemented our financial security and I handed in my notice at the office a month after the funeral.

I intend to faithfully record all the details, or *minutiae*, as Pamela might say, of my new life, with a view to passing on all my acquired knowledge in the not too distant future. I am drinking a glass of Bordeaux that has not travelled well and Pamela is measuring the windows for curtains. We have traditional Spanish shutters, I tell her, to no avail.

We bought this noble old house on the edge of the village in order to integrate more fully with the local people, while still keeping a generous plot of land for growing vegetables. I intend us to become self-sufficient in this respect and Pamela is all for me trying.

We were not attracted to the 'expat' life of sun and sangria, but to one of tilling the land, learning the language, and integrating. We are far enough away from the sea to avoid having English-speaking neighbours, I think. I searched thoroughly for the house on the internet and managed to push the price down considerably. I always drive a hard bargain and imagine that the estate agency I dealt with made very little, if any, profit. We got a lot of house and land for our money - far more than had we followed the droves down to the coast - and 'swimming pool' are two words that do not form part of my vocabulary - unless I use them separately, of course, or when referring to public bathing establishments or suchlike. Land is for production, not for swimming in.

Friday 2nd November

One hour of Spanish grammar duly studied before settling down with a glass of wine to write my journal. A different bottle but the same acidic taste. I wish I had left my modest wine reserve in the house on Swinburne Crescent now. The man who bought our house ogled it so, that had he not haggled in such a petty manner about the price, I would have made him a gift of it.

A young Scotch person called Andy came round this morning while I was in Villeda, the capital of the borough, sorting out paperwork with the interpreter, whose services I won't require for very much longer. I hoped that Pamela hadn't been *too* welcoming as she knows that I wish to avoid over-fraternisation (look up) with any foreign elements. She said that she hadn't, but that he had seemed very nice, and I said that I was sure that he was. She still insists on the curtains. I have started digging over the plot of land, as I intend to avoid the use of expensive and unnecessary machinery. It is very hard and dry and I only managed about a square yard. On the upside, there aren't many weeds to worry about. Sore hands now, making it difficult to hold the pen. I will make a more thorough journal entry tomorrow.

Saturday 3rd November

Raining today. Excellent news for the land! It should also make it easier to dig. The Scotsman called round again this morning with some eggs. When I asked him if he had grown them himself, Pamela burst out laughing. The Scotsman knew that I meant the hens and that I had used the verb loosely. He told me that he had several good layers and a feisty cock. It appears that he lives on a 'finca' just outside the village and has been here for eight years. I thanked him and he soon left.

After studying Spanish grammar for an hour, I looked over the paperwork for the house. It appears that the house and the plot are separate entities, although previously owned by the same person. The interpreter, who the Town Hall recommended, says that there are one or two small points to clear up regarding the land, but that I shouldn't worry. I won't worry. I'm not a worrier.

Pamela drove into town to do the weekly shop and also purchased a roll of material for the curtains. "Tasteful, but unnecessary," I said, and was ignored. Pamela is not as diligent in her grammar studies as I, but says that her knowing French will help. I don't see why it should, it being a different language, but she just said, "Espera y verás." I looked that up and it means 'wait and see'. I will revise the future tenses in bed tonight.

Sunday 4th November

Sunny again today and I resumed my digging, using gloves. I had little time for gardening in England and I will harden my hands little by little. The Scotsman called round and interrupted my work. He offered me the use of a small rotavator to plough the land, but I declined. He said it would take me weeks to do it by hand and I must say that yesterday's rain has not made it any easier to dig. The water must have rolled straight down the slope and onto the track - such a waste. The Scotsman's parting shot was, "piss on your hands," which I thought rather uncouth. Another square yard dug over.

After lunch I ventured to the village bar to have coffee, having checked the correct time to do so on the internet. Pamela offered to accompany me, but I insisted that we avoid going everywhere together and being considered 'that foreign couple'. The bar is very rustic and smoky and the customers, all men, were very attentive, I must say. They all looked at me as I entered and responded to my, "Buenas tardes," replying likewise or with friendly grunts and growls. They were all still looking at me as I ordered a coffee with milk in the correct manner. The young waiter seemed a little slow to respond - a little soft in the head, I suspect - but eventually produced the coffee, which was excellent. I drank my coffee at the bar, like a local, and noticed that I was still attracting considerable attention. The novelty of seeing a foreigner, I suppose, although I had made a point of wearing my espadrilles. Nobody else was wearing them, I noticed. I failed to strike up a conversation today, but will persevere. One hour of grammar after dinner.

Monday 5th November

Getting up time is an issue which I shall have to address. In my former life I arose at 6.35am midweek and at 7.55am on Saturdays and Sundays and I fully intended to adhere to those times here. I have *not* retired, but merely swapped the suit of the commuter for the rugged attire of one who intends to work the land and be as one with his rustic neighbours. Having said that, it was chilly this morning and I found myself pacing round the plot to keep warm until the sun appeared. Pamela has determined to rise no earlier than half past eight, which, as she always worked part-time and locally, will be no great wrench to her customs. Until the end of winter I shall rise every day at my weekend hour. This is not sloth, merely expediency.

Pamela returned from the village with our daily bread and told me she had met a lady from Essex. I must have looked downcast as she then told me that the lady and her 'partner' (meaning not married) only use their holiday home two or three times a year. Seeing me cheer up, Pamela then told me that the lady, Tracy by name, knew several more British couples who live in the area. This is not what I desired or expected and made me feel quite low while I was digging today's square yard. I only managed half an hour's grammar; prepositions - most confusing. I wish they would stick to the rules. I uncorked a bottle of wine that has survived the move, which cheered me up a bit, and the Scotsman didn't call round today.

Tuesday 6th November

When I returned from the Town Hall, I heard mechanical noises from the rear of the house and rushed through to catch the Scotsman *in fraglanti*, mechanically ploughing my plot with Pamela looking on, doing nothing to stop him. I was about to protest, but on seeing his lightening progress compared to me and my spade, I retreated unseen into the house and saved my remonstrations for when he had begun the last run up the slope. My feeble protests were a failure, as my joy upon seeing the beautifully churned up land obviously belied my stern expression. Pamela kissed me and Andy said that I could now stop pissing on my hands. I pointed out that I had never started and went to uncork another bottle of the well-travelled wine. If we must have one foreign friend, I suppose we could make a worse choice than Andy and, as a vote of confidence, I shall stop referring to him as 'The Scotsman' in this journal.

I shall now open my horticulture book and see what I can plant tomorrow.

Wednesday 7th November

I was up until 2 o'clock last night, translating unknown words from the horticulture book - about three-quarters of them. After breakfast, I took a cup of tea and a chair out to the terrace which looks onto the plot and tried to decide where to put the garlic, radishes, broad beans and onions that my book allows me to plant here in November. I may seek help from a knowledgeable local person, as I am not sure what part of each vegetable I should plant. The seeds? Little onions? Little beans? The book is not clear about this and I cannot find a local plant nursery on the internet, only ones for small children. Perhaps these people are still sufficiently in touch with the soil to have no need for such establishments. I will prepare my questions and ask the neighbours to our left, who I have yet to introduce myself to and have a well-tended plot. The neighbours to our right; a young, swarthy couple, spend all their time indoors, often with music playing, and have two old cars and other assorted junk on their plot. This is a shame and an eyesore. I will have words with them when I become more articulate in Spanish.

Thursday 8th November

Andy called round with some olives while I was sitting in the sun with my grammar book. I had been finding it difficult to concentrate on my irregular participles, as the beauty of my plot distracted me. The earth is beckoning my seed and I think that I am finding a long lost bondage with the land reawakening in my urbanised soul. (Good sentence, but find alternative to bondage.) I don't like olives, but I believe they are an acquired taste and I mean to acquire it. Likewise with garlic and olive oil. Also Spanish cheese, cured ham, dried cod, and anchovies.

I refrained from asking Andy's advice on horticultural matters, as I fear he may have considerable knowledge and impart it all to me in English. I would rather have it from the horse's mouth - meaning a Spanish peasant's mouth, and I don't mean peasant in a demeaning way. I am already preparing the questions that I intend to ask our neighbours to the left.

Pamela has been busy all day making up the curtains. They are of a greeny-white pattern and would certainly look very handsome in an English house. At least they match the shutters.

Friday 9th November

I called on the neighbours to our left this morning, an aged couple. I started in with, "Good morning. I am your new neighbour," (in Spanish) and they appeared to understand this. I then introduced myself and asked them how they were, using the formal 'Usted' pronoun as we are not yet close friends. They then introduced themselves and asked me how I was, and I responded correctly. He is called Nora - a strange name for a man and one which I shall look up - and she Angeles. ('Anggelees' - throat clearing sound on the 'g'.) Angeles then showed me round the entire house, upstairs and down, talking very quickly all the while. I understood her reasonably well, mainly through her gestures and facial expressions. I am discovering that reading Spanish and listening to it are very different things. On returning to the rustic living room, Nora took me in hand and led me through the very rustic kitchen to his plot. I took the list of questions from my shirt pocket and asked him what he was growing on his land. On retrospect, the question was a little foolish, as I could see the tomatoes, peppers, lettuces and cauliflowers from where we stood. He told me anyway, speaking much more slowly than his wife, almost as if I were an idiot, for which I was grateful (for him speaking slowly). He also pointed out where the potatoes, onions, garlic, carrots and something called 'nabos' had been sown and showed me his cherry, plum and almond trees. By this time, my brain was hurting through the sheer weight of foreign language being poured into it and I decided to save my specific questions for another day. During our final, somewhat one-way, exchange, I understood that Angeles is rather keen to meet Pamela and I indicated, through single words and arm movements, that she would soon call round.

A large glass of Bordeaux helped me to recover my senses and, once more serene, I smile as I write my journal. This has, after all, been a watershed day; my first real verbal intercourse with the people of my new country! 'Nabos' are turnips.

Saturday 10th November

Pamela called round to see Nora and Angeles this morning. I insisted that she went alone, in order to establish herself as herself and not just as 'the Englishman's wife' ('la inglesa esposa', I think) and she was more than happy to do so. She returned two hours later with Angeles and gave her a tour of the house. I followed at a discrete distance and listened to

Angeles's stream of unintelligible talk. Pamela responded occasionally with comments and questions, so she must have understood a few words.

I went to the bar for coffee with two conversation-starting phrases written on my hand: 'El tiempo es bonito' - 'The weather is nice,' and, 'Tengo 54 anos' - 'I am 54'. The same dim waiter smirked from within his smoke cloud when I ordered my coffee in the correct manner. I addressed my first phrase to a man dressed in blue overalls at the bar and I think he said that he wished for rain. I said, "Sí," because I too will need rain for my plot. On following up with my second phrase, he sprayed coffee from his mouth, had a fit of coughing, and rushed out of the bar. I was so concerned that I went to the door of the bar, only to see him driving away on his tractor, still coughing and bouncing up and down. Pamela pointed out later that 'ano' means anus; I had forgotten about the squiggly accent. She was kind enough not to laugh, knowing how much my Spanish means to me, so I also told her how I ordered the coffee. She thinks that a native would understand my question as, 'Can I possess a coffee?' but I am more concerned about the anus. I am almost sure that nobody else in the bar heard me. He drove a red tractor.

Sunday 11th November

Today was a better day than yesterday. Nora (short for Honorario - still strange) came round with a plastic bag and ushered me out to the plot. He showed me some beans and made a scrabbling motion. I brought the spade and he shook his head and left. He returned with what I took to be an extremely large hoe and said, "asada, asada" (spelt 'azada' I later discovered). He started to scrape out a furrow and gave me a thumbs up sign. I returned the thumbs up sign, but wish he had asked me where I wanted to plant the beans. He placed three beans in the furrow, making exaggerated motions with his hands and nodding. He covered the beans, nodding and smiling at me all the while. He did not speak throughout the process and I still think he thinks I am an idiot. I said 'bien' several times to show that I am not. I may turn to Andy for future guidance as at least he will let me choose where to place each item. When Nora left, with a short 'adiós', I completed the furrow - approximately twenty-two yards long - and felt like my own man again. I will buy my own 'azada', and a trowel too.

Angeles came to help Pamela with the curtains and kept up a constant stream of chatter - quite the opposite of her husband. Pamela says she is bossy, but is good for her listening comprehension. I said that Nora is good for my miming comprehension, which I thought rather funny. One and a half hours of grammar. No sign of Andy today.

Monday 12th November

Andy called round this morning and responded to my, "Long time no see," with, "I didn't want you to think I was an interfering f**ker." When he sees that I don't swear, he will soon stop blaspheming in my presence, I think. He had brought some beans in a bag and I showed him the furrow. He said it was long but straight. I think he meant too long, but that is a question of taste. We decided together where to plant the garlic, radishes and onions. He said it was a bit late for potatoes, but I will give them a go anyway. We decided together where to plant some trees. He suggested a couple each of cherry, plum and pear trees to begin with, and that he had some one-year-olds I could transplant. I offered to pay him for them but he refused, so it is not true what they say about Scotsmen; not this one anyway. Andy is married to a local lady called Ana, which is good news. He refers to her as 'Ella indoors', and it is true that we have yet to meet her.

One hour of grammar, followed by some sentence practice on Pamela. I am astonished at how much Spanish she knows, although she always was a clever woman. Some people have a gift for languages and it is too early to say if I have that gift too.

Martes 13th Noviembre

I will change the date back to English before the journal is published, to cater for uninitiated readers, as well as polishing up my prose and removing this sentence. The Red Tractor was outside my usual bar, so I tried the other one. My saying, "Póngame un café con leche, por favor," went down very well, although saying, 'Put me a coffee with milk, please,' sounds very odd to me. I don't know how they can justify such a construction, grammatically speaking. It did, however, produce a stream of questions from the fat, friendly young waitress, which I tried my best to respond to. I understood words like 'casa' and 'pueblo' and feel that I am making some progress, although I still need to make much use of my arms and face to make myself understood. The bar also seems a little more civilised - it has a sit down toilet - and less full of smoke than the other one. I may make it my 'local'.

I have just realised that Pamela is doing all the shopping and thus benefiting from increased verbal intercourse. She says that I may go to purchase the bread each day from now on. I am getting to grips with the azada and did one furrow gloveless. I planted the garlic cloves as Andy indicated and, by the time it is ready, I will have acquired a taste for it, I am sure.

One hour of grammar (past simple) and more sentence testing with Pamela. I will avoid questions for now, as they produce long, rapid answers which I don't understand. Even asking the girl at the bar if she lived here produced a torrent of words. It was, I thought, a very simple question.

No Andy or Nora today, although Angeles talked Pamela through two curtains. Pamela says she finds her tiresome but useful. I thought they were becoming good friends, but am rather glad they might not be. Angeles's voice penetrates all walls.

Miércoles, 14 de Noviembre (sic)

Another sunny day, but quite cold this morning. It will soon be time to try out the wood-burning stove. Pamela had suggested we install central heating, but I felt it was not necessary in this mild climate. Nora called round this morning as I was planting potatoes and shook his finger and grasped his arms around his body to imply cold. He appears to have lost the power of speech, although I heard him talking to Pamela in the kitchen. He disapproves of my long row of beans (shaking of head, arms in the air), but I don't see what difference it makes. Probably a question of asthetics (check spelling). I hope it will rain soon and water my plot.

Andy called round with the one-year-old trees and invited us to lunch on Saturday. Our first visit and a semi-native one, as his wife is not a foreigner! I planted the plum trees without gloves and watered the beans with the watering can, making several trips. I will buy a hosepipe next time I am in town. One hour of adjectives.

Jueves, 15 de Noviembre

Colder this morning. I went to the bakery to buy the bread; long 'barras' of bread; the sliced bread is awful anyway. The bakery was full of women and there was no queue, so I did not know where to stand. Another woman came in and asked a question and several ladies pointed at me. I felt quite self-conscious, being the only man present and not understanding the question. Yet another woman came in and asked the same question and the previous woman said, "Yo," (meaning 'I', or 'me'). This formula was repeated by each new arrival until I finally deduced that they were asking who was last in the 'queue'. Pamela, who has more shopping experience than I, says that this is standard procedure. It will take some getting used to, but at least you can move freely around the shop while you wait. It relies more on honesty than on maintaining a fixed physical position and, as soon as you are no longer the last person ('el último'), you can relax. It wouldn't work in London.

Pamela has almost finished sewing the curtains and says that her patience with Angeles is also coming to an end. She is now fed up, she says, of hearing about her grandchildren and of her own comments being ignored. Pamela is very patient; one of the most patient people I know, so she must be being tried very sorely. Angeles also walks in without knocking, which may or may not be the custom here, but is unsettling all the same, especially when she is wearing her pink dressing gown and matching flip-flops.

I planted the radishes where Andy and I had decided, and watered them. No rain or any sign of rain on the internet. One hour of adverbs - quite easy.

Viernes, 16 de Noviembre

Cold and sunny again this morning, so I decided to try lighting the wood-burning stove. I brought in some logs that had been left on the terrace by the previous owner, before realising that I had no kindling of any description. The logs were practically weightless and crumbled in my hands, so when I went for my post-lunch coffee in the clean bar, I told the waitress that I wanted some wood. "Quiero madera," were my actual words, but she looked perplexed, so I did such miming of wood chopping and fire lighting that I felt quite like Nora. She said, "Ah! Quieres leña!" and gave me a card for the wood supplier in Spanish, English and German; most disappointing. So there are different words for wood for making things out of, and firewood, which I consider annoying and unnecessary. Pamela rang the number on the card and, at my request, ordered the firewood in Spanish.

Pamela also pointed out that we have no television. I said that I was aware of this and she said that it would be useful for practising our listening comprehension. I agreed that this was so, but she then gave her true intentions away by telling me that Andy had a satellite dish. Having weaned her off EastEnders, which she is far too well-read to watch, I put my foot down most firmly. I agreed to the television, but not to the satellite dish, and she acquiesced. I hope this is not the thin end of one of Pamela's wedges. Pamela can be cunning and thinks she knows how to 'play' me. I am not as obtuse as she says I sometimes seem.

Sábado, 17 de Novienbre

Sunny yet again. This is fine for the expats, but not for a man, and his wife, wishing to live off the land. I planted the onions and the cherry and pear trees this morning. I made a lot of trips with the watering can and my arms were heavy on the steering wheel as we drove to Andy's.

Andy's wife, Ana, is very pretty and greeted us in Spanish, which I appreciated. They live in a lovely bungalow surrounded by land and outhouses, and keep four goats, three pigs, many hens and some cocks. They have an abundance of fruit and nut trees (expand on this when know names of them), olive trees, and a huge vegetable plot.

Ana had made a traditional Sunday roast - on a Saturday - and, although I would have preferred Spanish fare, it was delicious. The conversation moved imperceptibly into English as we ate, and I must say that Andy is a very lucky man; as lucky as I. Ana is a schoolteacher in Villeda and Andy tends the finca and does occasional odd jobs of an agricultural nature. Andy was quiet and well-mannered during the lunch and allowed his better half to host proceedings. He has made a very good match, although I see that I have implied this already.

After lunch, Andy took me on a tour of the finca while Ana and Pamela chatted over the washing up. He said that the goats had names, as they were milch goats, but the pigs did not, as they were 'for scoffing'. He pointed out the next one to be slaughtered and invited us to attend. He said that Ana's father would 'stick the bugger' and also said that I would find the whole slaughtering and post-slaughter activity instructive. I said I was sure that I would, and accepted the invitation. As a lifelong meat-eater, I cannot be squeamish about such things. The doomed pig was very friendly and seemed to smile.

This is the longest entry so far, and justly so. I must record all significant details for future readers. A journal is not a mere diary. I am sleepy now (6.32pm) after the heavy lunch, but it is too late for a siesta, which I haven't learnt how to take yet, but will. Commuters don't take siestas, although some do doze off on the train, always seeming to wake up moments before their stop. Uncanny (and irrelevant).

Domingo, 18 de Noviembre

It hasn't rained now for two weeks and is becoming a cause for concern. I saw Nora over the wall and he mimed at great length the lack of and need for rain. When we invite them to dinner, which Pamela says we must do, like it or not, I may suggest a game of charades. My manual watering is improving my upper-body strength, but it takes me two hours to get round all the items on my plot, and by the time I have finished, the first furrows are dry again. Am I penetrating to my seeds, cloves, roots etc.? I don't know. I will get a hosepipe tomorrow when I go into town. Pamela also wants me to look for some curtain rails and gave me measurements. I told her that I doubt that they exist in this country of window shutters, but that I will try. Half an hour of conjunctions and half an hour of horticultural and curtain vocabulary.

Lunes, 19 de Noviembre

I drove into town alone this morning as Pamela will go in to do the weekly shop tomorrow. The internet told me that the 'Ferretería' is the place to go for hardware and all sundry things that you cannot buy in other shops. I parked my car - a Spanish model - on a side street and asked the first person I saw for directions to a 'Ferretería', remembering to roll the double 'r' by making the tongue vibrate. I find that either no 'r's or about seven come out. I practise with important words like 'perro' (dog) and 'barra' (bar, stick) and will improve 'poco a poco' (little by little). If this journal were not intended for publication in the English-speaking world, I would probably find it turning 'poco a poco' into Spanish!

I followed the directions correctly and found my way to the large 'Ferretería'. The long counter was like that of a bar and men lolled on it as if it *were* a bar. There was no queue and, when I asked who the 'último' was, one man shrugged and turned his back on me. The four assistants moved very leisurely and listened patiently to the men's lengthy requests. The old man next to me flourished a small, rusty hinge and talked for an age while opening it, closing it, spitting on it and twisting it. The assistant eventually produced quite a different hinge and the man left happily. My request for 'railes de cortina' was not understood and much miming ensued. He finally produced a long wooden pole with some rings on, which I bought. Hosepipe requested correctly and supplied.

Pamela, after spending many hours sewing on traditional curtain hooks, which she says I must have seen her doing, was not impressed by the pole and the rings and immediately sat down at the computer to order some curtain rails from B&Q. The postage would be expensive, I told her, and added that I would find a use, probably horticultural, for the pole and rings.

An hour of present tense - mere revision.

Martes, 20 de Noviembre

Rain at last! I sat under the little veranda on the terrace, watching the rain soak into the ground and preparing some sentences to say to Nora. I intend to confront his miming with a barrage of topical, well-constructed phrases. I ran the sentences past Pamela and we made some minor adjustments. After a light lunch, I returned to the terrace to learn them off by heart. At the time of writing I have memorised seven, which are (in English):

The rain is good for the plants.

Spanish bread is good, but goes hard quickly.

In England I worked in an office.

My friend Andy is Scottish.

I used to play golf, but have given it up.

I like Spanish people.

My wife, Pamela, is a good cook.

This last sentence is to be closely followed by an invitation to dinner on Friday night. I practised reciting my lines to Pamela as she cleaned the kitchen, until she silenced me by saying that she hoped I hadn't forgotten that she wanted a television. I haven't forgotten.

Miércoles, 21 de Noviembre

Still raining! Great news, but has made for a dreary day. I revised my sentences in the morning and went to my usual bar for coffee. I was dismayed to find two uncouth, tattooed, bevested (look up) Englishmen drinking beer at the bar and talking at the tops of their voices. I sidled into a corner and picked up the Spanish newspaper, to no avail, as one of them hollered, "you English, pal?" I could but nod, and they were around me in a flash with their beery breath and northern accents. How they knew I was English, I do not know. They - Gary and Mark by name - are builders and are "makin' a killing doin' up Brits' 'ouses" (Gary's words, not mine). They asked me if I needed any building work doing and I told them that my house was in first class shape when I bought it (which was true) and that I always dealt with local tradesmen (which is not, yet). I left as soon as I had finished my coffee and am sure that I heard one of them say 'snotty f**ker' when I reached the street.

Feeling low as I write this. Not due to meeting riff-raff, but to the fact that they have a lot of work with other 'Brits'. I will invite Nora and Angeles to dinner tomorrow - we have to start our integration process somewhere.

Jueves, 22 de Noviembre

More rain. I revised my sentences, adding 'It's raining cats and dogs' as an opener, before calling on our neighbours. I wished them, "Buenos días," and, without giving them a chance to speak or mime, I said, "Está lloviendo gatos y perros." Their reaction was unexpected. Angeles said, "Gatos? perros? gatos? perros?" countless times, while Nora barked and shook his head. I had no stomach for my remaining phrases and silenced them with my dinner invitation. This was comprehended but refused. We, I understood, are to come to lunch with them tomorrow. I agreed and left.

Pamela thought that it did not rain cats and dogs in Spanish. She looked up the equivalent phrase, which means 'raining pitchers' or 'raining jugs', and told me that idiomatic expressions are different in each language. She then told me what idiomatic expressions are.

The last two days have not been easy ones for me. 'Slings and arrows' seem to have been coming at me thick and fast. I didn't expect the transition to Spanish life to be easy, so I will grin and bear it. I may be grinning and bearing a lot at lunch with Nora and Angeles tomorrow.

Viernes, 23 de Noviembre

The rain continues. Three weeds have appeared on the plot, but I can't get at them, as the soil is so completely saturated. I must purchase some wellington boots, something I did not think I would ever need here. The internet informs me that the rain will cease this afternoon. I revised my sentences before going next door. I added 'the rain will stop this afternoon' to my repertoire.

The lunch was more a success than a failure. From a culinary point of view, I was able to face and partially conquer my demons. I battled through my share of the oil and vinegar-drenched salad and ate four olives. I ate two slices of cured ham, with bread. Angeles had made a paella (difficult to say properly: 'payelya') over a wood fire in the yard, which was very rustic and tasty. I squeezed a garlic clove with my fork and ate the contents to no ill effect. I can still taste it now, despite having cleaned my teeth twice. From a conversational point of view, the lunch was a great success. I doggedly inserted my phrases into Angeles's babble, and Pamela was kind enough to follow them up and, as she said later, "put them into some sort of context." Nora mimed somewhat less, but is still unable to address me directly. 'Poco a poco' he will come round.

I am feeling much cheered this evening as I sip a glass from the last of the unruined bottles. I can now stock up on Riojas and other fine Spanish wines!

Sábado, 24 de Noviembre

A sunny day and very warm by Spanish, and our, lunchtime - 2pm. This morning I was able to pad across the still soggy plot in my espadrilles and pick the weeds (7). I wanted to do some gardening work, but there is nothing to do but wait. I can almost feel my seeds germinating! My hosepipe is not yet operational, as I forgot to buy the thing that connects it to the tap. I have added it to my 'Ferretería' list.

Feeling emotionally strong after yesterday's successful lunch, I decided to have coffee in the 'campesino' (peasant: non-derogatory) bar again. The Red Tractor was outside, but I did not flinch. I entered, sat down next to the tractor owner at the bar, and said to him, "Tengo 54 años" ('anyyyos' - to leave no room for doubt). He said, "bien, bien," shook my hand, and ordered me a 'café con leche'. I followed up with some of my stock phrases and he responded in an agreeable manner (70/30: speech/mime - an acceptable ratio). He shook my hand warmly again as I left. He was in no hurry to leave as he is probably experiencing the same dearth of agricultural labours to do as myself. This fruitful encounter shows that the forthright, confident approach is the way forward in my quest for integration. 'Don't be shy, Ernest,' will be my motto!

Pamela tells me that she got into conversation with a local lady she met at the bakery, me having forgotten to go, who then invited her back to her house for coffee and more chatter. I don't feel that I can actually 'chat' yet, but I am pleased for her. We each blaze our independent integration trails, which will no doubt intertwine at some point, as the village - of 424 'habitantes', the internet tells me - is small.

Domingo, 25 de Noviembre

A sunny day and the first appearance of a bean sprout! While I was delighting in this, I saw the right-hand neighbour in his plot/scrapyard for the first time. He was talking on a mobile telephone and smoking what I suspected to be a 'joint'. Despite this, I waved and said, "Hola." He waved back absently before retreating indoors. I mentioned this encounter to Pamela, who I know partook of the occasional 'joint' at university, but not since meeting me, and she said, "Each to their own." I am still not altogether happy about this revelation and hope he does not consume other more heinous drugs as well. There are only three houses on our row and, if a third of them are already disreputable, I fear the worst. Nora and Angeles will hopefully live for a long time yet.

I have added three questions to my stock of phrases:

'Have you lived here long?'

'What do you do?' and,

'Have you planted much this year?'

When I feel that my phrases are going down well, I will insert a question and hope that I understand the answer. I spent half an hour eliciting different answers to these questions from Pamela, until she tired of it and put on Beethoven's Ninth quite loudly.

Lunes, 26 de Noviembre

A cloudy day. The beans are now sprouting in force and I believe the potatoes are breaking through too! The internet tells me that the radishes should also be making an appearance, but they have not done so yet. I removed some new weeds after a breakfast of 'tostadas' (toast) with butter and jam. This is typical Spanish breakfast fare and will replace the Weetabix which has run out. We had already finished the Branston Pickle, brown sauce, cheddar cheese and Marks & Spencer salad dressing, and I am glad. I have forbidden Pamela from buying any of these foreign articles on the internet. ('Forbidden' is too strong, and inaccurate, a word. Change for, 'urged her not to buy.')

I drove into town and made a beeline for the 'Ferretería'. Before taking my place at the crowded counter, I toured the aisles and began to wish that I hadn't insisted on the house being restored to the very highest standard; a requirement forming part of the extremely hard bargain that I drove. There are so many things that I would like to buy, doorknobs for one, but cannot justify. I bought the coupling for the hosepipe, a pair of wellington boots, a screwdriver, a torch, and some tape, but I will return with a better list.

Today at the counter an old man was flourishing a small bulb and waxing lyrical. The assistant nodded politely for about two minutes and then bobbed down quickly and produced a new bulb. The old man was cut off in mid-flow, took some coppers from his purse and laid them on the counter, and trudged out. Perhaps there is a time limit for each person. I already had all my items, so I quickly composed a phrase: "These wellington boots are good for the rain," but only received a blank stare. I will hover near another assistant next time.

Pamela tells me that she has been chatting with her new friend again today. I need a friend to chat to. Ninety minutes of miscellaneous grammar and I also practised my double-Rs in front of the mirror. Pamela asked me why I was calling myself a dog, so I must have been getting it right.

Martes, 27 de Noviembre

A cold night and a cold, sunny morning. Pamela complained

of this and, as if by chance, the wood supplier ('hombre de leña?') arrived! He brought large logs, smaller logs and kindling, and dumped it all outside the front door. The price was not low but there is a large amount, which I am sure will last us through the short winter. In this respect, it is not expensive. I spent the whole morning carrying the wood through the house to the sheltered part of the terrace. Pamela seems to have resumed bread buying duties, as it is at the bakery where she meets her new friend. She was out for two hours; two whole hours of integration! I am a little 'piqued', but must not hold her back. I went to the rustic bar for coffee, but my tractor driving friend was not there. Nobody seemed willing to converse, so I read the paper for a while. I understand more and more, but it is just not the same as speech.

I lit the wood-burning stove this evening after creating a structure of paper, kindling and medium logs, from the bottom up. At the third attempt and the second rebuild, it took hold, briefly filled the 'salón' with smoke, and then began to produce a remarkable heat. Pamela was impressed, but said that we did not sleep in the living room. I pointed out that our bedroom lay directly above and would feel the effects. She went upstairs and returned to say that the floor was cold to the touch. These old houses are very well-built! One hour of useful but boring grammar in bed. Pamela said she was too tired to respond to my utterances and that she had had enough Spanish for one day, thus this late journal entry to illustrate the support that I receive from my wife.

Miércoles, 28 de Noviembre

I awoke with Pamela's last words still lodged in my mind and, while weeding, had an 'eureka' moment. Classes! I would pay someone to talk and listen to me, and I told Pamela this as she was getting ready to go on her linguistic bakery outing. She reminded me that I dislike spending money (not wholly true) and suggested that I find someone with whom to have exchange classes. In an exchange class, Pamela says, you listen to someone waffling on in English for half an hour and then inflict the same torture on them for half an hour in their language (i.e.: Spanish). She says it is best to get the English out of the way first, if possible. It turns out that she partook of these classes during her year in Paris; a year which she has told me very little about. She may have smoked 'joints' then too, for all I know.

I typed out an advert on the computer in English - they will have to know some English - and pinned up a copy in both bars, the bakery, and a small windowless grocer's shop that I have discovered. The body of the advert reads:

Englishman seeks Spanish speaker for 'Exchange Classes'.
You will speak English for half a hour (30 minutes) and I will correct you.
I will then speak Spanish for half an hour and you will correct me.
I am patient and so must you be with me.
Venue to be convenient to both parties.
No monies to be exchanged.

I think this outlines the purpose and the method of the classes to good effect. At the time of writing, no-one has yet responded.

Studied one hour of grammar and did not trouble Pamela with any of my new sentences.

Jueves, 29 de Noviembre

A sunny day after a cool night. I am sure our ten tog (spring/autumn) duvet will suffice for what remains of the winter. After weeding, I reconnoitred the house with my notepad, looking for things that can be improved and jotting down essential items to be purchased at the 'Ferretería'. I concluded that I require: fire-lighters, matches, a toothbrush holder, spare bulbs, adhesive foam strips for windows and doors, two doorstops, an electric drill, screws and plastic plugs, a hammer, nails, pliers, sandpaper, wood varnish, white, black and green paint, brushes and turpentine. I may divide this into two lists, as I do so enjoy my 'Ferretería' trips.

I saw the swarthy neighbour on his 'plot' again before lunch. He was smoking a normal cigarette and drinking a can of coke. Today he addressed me and said, "Tú conoces a Andy, no?" which I understood to mean; rightly, I later found, 'You know Andy, don't you?' I quickly replied, "Sí," and he said, "Buen tío, buen tío!" which I later found to mean, 'Good uncle, good uncle'. How Andy has come to know that unsavoury specimen, to whom it appears he might even be related, I do not know. He did provide me with a short conversational exchange, though, and I will not reject his advances for the time being.

I had lunch alone, as Pamela had informed me that she was lunching with her new friend, and took coffee in the clean bar. I pointed to my advert and gave a 'thumbs up' sign to the fat young waitress.

She said, "En el pueblo nadie habla inglés," and I understood her!

(For the uninitiated: 'In the village nobody speaks English.')

I replied, "No?" and she said, "No".

I then said, "Y tú?" and she said, "No, no, no, no!"

I was happy to have taken part in a conversation, but disappointed that I may not find a suitable exchange student here in the village.

Pamela was not impressed by my 'Ferretería' list, said we did not need the paint and the varnish, and accused me of getting bored. I told her that 'boredom' was not in my vocabulary and went off to translate my 'Ferretería' list. It is not unusual for us to have these 'cool' periods and she always comes round eventually.

Viernes, 30 de Noviembre

Pamela has come round. She tells me that her friend's husband may well be interested in the exchange classes and that we are to have coffee with them at their home tomorrow. This is good news! I asked her if they were cultured people and she said, "Cultured enough." I did not enquire further, as beggars cannot be choosers.

Andy called round at midday with some eggs and would not accept payment. I would like to return his favours in some way, but imagine he is more accomplished at all the things that people do around here than I am. I could do his tax returns, but not in Spanish. I now regret not being more 'handy', and to having preferred golf to D.I.Y., but I shall soon take to it. Golf, needless to say, is now a thing of the past, being the one activity that *would* have me labelled 'expat'! I mentioned that the swarthy neighbour had mentioned him, and he just said that he knew everybody in the village. I did not pursue the matter or comment on his vile habits. (The neighbour's.)

Coffee in the rustic bar. No tractor man. I alerted those present to my advert and received jovial negatives all round. I expected no less in *that* bar, but to provoke laughter was gratifying in itself and shows that they are beginning to accept me.

I weeded in the failing light - 6pm – and failed to see any sign of the radishes. One hour of grammar; my first dabble with the subjunctive tense. I don't think I am going to enjoy it and don't see any need for it. English does very well without it, and is the world's number one language, if you don't count Chinese.

Sábado, 1 de DICIEMBRE 2007

Early morning drizzle, clearing up by midday. One month ago today I began this journal! It seems like an age and at the same time it seems like yesterday. The vegetable plot is well under way, though still mostly underground, and my Spanish is progressing satisfactorily, while also remaining mostly 'underground', in the sense that the roots of my grammatical base will soon push up conversational shoots which will later blossom into flowers of eloquence. (Fine sentence.)

The new month has begun with a surprise, and a very pleasant one. Who should Pamela's new friend's husband be, but my friend the tractor man!! We called round at their tidy home at half past three, and our mutual delight on recognition led us to embrace and pat each other on the back heartily, something I have seldom done before. He is called Paco and Pamela's friend is called Laura. Laura is a polite, plain lady of forty. She is less rustic than Paco and wore formal shoes in the house, while Paco, preferring not to stand on ceremony, went barefoot.

Laura explained to us over coffee that Paco was inordinately fond of Country and Western music and wished to understand what they were saying. Paco nodded vigorously and, by way of illustration, put on a Johnny Cash recording and sang along in a remarkable way to 'Ring of Fire', running each word strangely and seamlessly into the next. He also mimed the trumpet playing in a manner that Nora would have been proud of. I asked Pamela to ask him how much of the song he understood and he confessed to only understanding the words 'of' and 'fire'. I saw that I had a mighty task on my hands, as Paco's English is much more rudimentary than my Spanish. I explained that 'gramática' was very 'importante' and Paco nodded happily, before producing some small glasses and a bottle of ice-cold almond liqueur. We toasted to our linguistic venture and agreed to start on Monday evening at our house.

Our second month has started auspiciously and I approve of Pamela's new friend, who appears to be very steady and sensible. Pamela is easily led astray, as she once was by a supposed 'clairvoyant' woman, and I feel she is in safe hands with Laura. I spent one hour working on material for Paco's first class.

Domingo, 2 de Diciembre

A warm, cloudy day and no need to light the wood-burning stove. I shouldn't be surprised if the winter passes us by without us noticing. The weeds are well under control, but no benign growth has appeared as yet. I have sketched out a rudimentary syllabus for Paco's English studies. Grammar is the key, as I myself know, and Country and Western lyrics will have to wait until he grasps the basic concepts. As for my half of the class, I intend to ask Paco a series of questions in the hope that a conversation will ensue. Pamela has warned me not to be overambitious and not to convert this into one of my 'crazes'. I insisted that a 54 year old man does not have 'crazes', but carefully weighs up how to spend his time to best effect. She replied that a forty-something year old man she once knew had had a golf craze, a jogging craze, a model railway craze and a coin collecting craze all in the space of five years. I am no longer, I said, such a man, and that golf was much more than a craze.

As language analysis has filled my day, I had no desire to struggle with subjunctives in the evening, and instead read some Wodehouse over a glass or two of the Valdepeñas white that Pamela had bought at the supermarket. Both the wine and the Wodehouse were very palatable.

Lunes, 3 de Diciembre

Overcast. After watering with my new hosepipe, I strolled around the village to kill time before my much anticipated class with Paco. I called in at the windowless grocer's shop and browsed for a long time before an elderly lady came through a small door to attend me. She eyed me suspiciously, as if I were a shoplifter or an alien, so I bought a dusty bottle of almond liqueur to allay her suspicions. She pocketed my money, croaked a curt, "Adiós," and shuffled back through her door. An alien then, as I could have 'cleaned out' the shop.

Paco rolled up on his tractor just before seven and I showed him through to the room that is to become my study. We began with Paco's half hour of English and when he produced a Patsy Cline CD I said, "hoy no," (not today) and he obediently put it back in his pocket. I began by introducing him to the verb 'To be', taking him through the six conjugations in turn. I made the mistake of writing them down for him and his initial efforts of "Ee aam, yow arr, hee ees, chee ees" etc., showed me the error of my ways. By the time I had untaught him this and taught him the correct pronunciation, it was time for my half hour of Spanish.

I opened proceedings by asking him, "What do you do?" (in Spanish, of course). He said that he was sitting here. I said, "no, what do you *do*?" (¿Qué *haces*?) and he said he was listening to me. As he had obviously misunderstood the question, I asked and answered the question myself several times with appropriate mimes ('I am a fireman, I am a doctor, I am an accountant,' and so on). He finally understood and told me that he was indeed an 'agricultor'. That settled, I asked him if he had lived here long. He answered that he did not live here, but on Calle Ancha (Wide Street) and, before I had time to clarify, he pointed at his watch and clasped his head to signify, I think, that his brain was full. Why he also found the Spanish part of the class difficult, I do not know. I brought out the almond liqueur; very tasty when taken cold, and we wound down with a little Patsy Cline.

Our very first exchange class was, I believe, a qualified success. We covered very little material, but did break the ice and lay the foundations for what is to be the structure of our classes. I did have my doubts about Paco's correct usage of the Spanish language, but Pamela later pointed out to me that they often use the present simple tense as the present continuous and that they use quite a different question for asking a person's occupation. Why they cannot use each tense in the correct manner, I do not know.

Martes, 4 de Diciembre

Rain today, so I needn't have watered yesterday. I took the first half of my list to the 'Ferretería' and was delighted to find all the items on the shelves, except the toothbrush holder. I made the most of my two minutes grace at the counter to explain what I required (60/40: mime/speech) and the assistant, a different one today, but equally blank-faced, reached below the counter and produced a glass. I said I already had several of those and paid for my other items. A glass, it is true, would do the job.

I prepared Paco's second class - how to make use of the verb 'to be' - and lamented that Spanish has two equivalent verbs to our one. Why? There is no need for it and it simply leads to confusion. I later surveyed my study and decided on what I would need in order to make it more study-like. At present there is a table, two chairs, one bookcase, a small CD player and a bin. I will need a proper desk, more bookcases and shelves, and books. Our present collection, which looked so large in the boxes, is quite unimpressive. I will expand my library with both English and Spanish books 'poco a poco'.

Miércoles, 5 de Diciembre

Sunny again, and a cold start to the day. Pamela insisted that I light the wood-burning stove as she was lunching in today. I asked her if she was tiring of her new friend Laura and she replied that she was not, and that she wished I would stop referring to her as her 'new friend', as she was now an established friend. I duly lit the stove with one of my new fire-lighters and, after the initial smoke, it soon roared away merrily. Pamela made a nice tuna salad for lunch and I applied a little olive oil and vinegar 'a la española'. It tasted less horrible than last time. I shall buy Pamela a Spanish cookbook when I am next in town, as we will have to wean ourselves off

Shepherd's Pie, Lancashire Hot Pot, Italian Lasagne, Indian Curry, et al.

I made some final adjustments to my material for Paco's class tomorrow and wrote some new questions in Spanish:

Do you like fish/meat/snails etc.?

Would you like to go to (insert place)?

Where can I buy a toothbrush holder?

I hope Paco is looking forward to the class as much as I am! Perhaps we should extend it to forty-five minutes each. I will ask him tomorrow.

Jueves, 6 de Diciembre

A cold, clear morning and Pamela once again required me to light the wood-burning stove. It consumed a surprising amount of wood yesterday, as I kept it 'ticking over' all day. I soon had it relit, thanks to the magical fire-lighters. Pamela has made it very clear that the manning of the stove is to be my job, as it was I who had got cold feet over installing central heating. I did not demur and we both laughed at her unintentional joke.

Paco's arrival at seven set the front door rattling. He must really enjoy driving around on his little old tractor as the village can be covered on foot from end to end in less than three minutes. I was most disappointed to find that he had forgotten five-sixths of his 'to be' studies. With a little prompting he was able to say 'I am Paco' and within ten minutes we had added 'You are Ernest' to his repertoire. I thought about explaining the pun which can be derived from my name, as in the Oscar Wilde play, but decided to leave that for a later date. I produced three photographs: of my Uncle

Roger, of Pamela's cousin Felicity, and of a Yorkshire Terrier that Uncle Roger once owned, in order to practice the third person singular. (For the uninitiated: he is, she is, it is.)

For simplicity, I changed the names to Bill, Susan and Scamp, before proceeding to name them. Paco was more interested in who they really were than in saying 'she is Susan, it is Scamp' etc., and by the end of the thirty minutes he only had a shaky grasp of the grammar involved. With relief I began my thirty minutes by asking him, in Spanish, if he liked fish. He said that he did and I asked him to ask me a similar question. He stuck stolidly to fish and asked me if I liked several different kinds, which required much use of the dictionary. By the end of the class I knew how to say, and like, hake, trout, plaice, cod and sea bass. I brought out the almond liqueur, while Paco put on a Conrad Twitty CD, and we unwound to the sound of Country and Western music at its best.

Our second class then, while also a qualified success, only increased my knowledge and that of Paco by the tiniest fraction. I only taught about 10% of the material I had prepared for Paco, and myself learnt the names of four fish, as I knew cod already. My suggestion of increasing the class time produced much head clasping, and I begin to feel that Paco does not possess the same motivation as I. Some rethinking is to be done, methinks.

Viernes, 7 de diciembre

A warmer day, so there was no need to light the wood-burning stove. I cleaned it out, covering the floor with dust as I did so, and Pamela handed me the dustpan and brush. Everything pertaining to the stove, she says, is my responsibility. I was dismayed to witness the arrival of the curtain fixtures, an awful lot of them, as I would be expected to put them up. I cheered up when I remembered that I now embrace all things D.I.Y. and that it may also warrant more trips to the Ferretería. I have now dropped the apostrophes around Ferretería as the word now forms part of my everyday vocabulary. 'Hardware Store' sounds dull in comparison, and rather American.

While weeding and inspecting my shoots, Nora appeared, having smoked his pipe all the way through the house. I will have to speak to him about this, as Pamela and I are both fervent non-smokers. I alerted him to the progress of the beans and potatoes and he shook his head over the latter, making a small circle between his thumb and forefinger. I took this to mean that the future potatoes would be small. I pointed out that the radishes had not sprouted and he drew his finger across his throat. Nora's negative attitude is beginning to annoy me.

Sábado, 8 de diciembre

Today is a national holiday in honour of the Virgin of the Immaculate Conception. People cannot be pleased that the holidays falls on a Saturday, but I don't suppose they can shift it to Monday if she conceived 2007 years ago today. Her pregnancy was certainly a short one. Papist nonsense, anyway. Pamela and I are staunch C. of E. non-churchgoers.

Andy called round with some goat's cheese and invited us to a barbecue tomorrow. The weather forecast was good, he said, and some friends would be coming up from the coast. I shuddered at the word 'coast' and asked if they were English. He said that they were most certainly not. There would be one or two English people present, but there would be a good mix of nationalities, he said. Pamela accepted the invitation on our behalf. I will mingle with the Spanish guests.

Domingo, 9 de Diciembre

A bright day and quite warm in the sun. A far cry from England in December! The pleasure that the wonderful day brought me was soon checked when we arrived at Andy and Ana's and met the other barbecue invitees. The two English builders who I had met in the bar were there, along with an Irish couple and a contingent of Scottish people from the coast. The only Spanish guest was Ana's cousin Beatriz, who is deaf. Pamela circulated freely while I politely entertained Ana, who looked lovely in a pale blue dress, and her cousin. My recent miming requirements enabled me to communicate with Beatriz just as well as I have been doing with other Spanish people, which, on reflection, says little for my verbal skills.

We ate heartily of pork chops, sausages, and a black sausage that reminds me very much of black pudding without the revolting smell. The Anglo-Saxons all started drinking right away, including Pamela, and were soon being boisterous and uncouth. I too decided to have a glass or two to make the event more bearable, so when Gary the builder later slapped me on the back and said, "Alreet, matey," I was able to conceal my distaste to some extent. Mark, the other builder, repeated the offer of their services and I once again declined, more graciously than the previous time, I think. We do have to live alongside these people, after all. The Scots had brought a portable karaoke machine and, towards the end of the afternoon, I was induced to give a rendition of 'New York, New York', which was applauded raucously. When night drew in, we repaired indoors and played a game of charades at which, Pamela said, I excelled. After some Irish songs and Scottish dancing, Ana drove us home at eleven.

Lunes, 10 de Diciembre

I feel obliged to confess to my future readers that I wrote all but the first three words of yesterday's entry this morning. The spirit of the occasion made me too weary to write last night. Pamela says that I appear to have 'changed my tune' about consorting with other British (and Irish) people, but I pointed out that, given the lack of natives, I merely strove to adapt to circumstances. Pamela said I had adapted extremely thoroughly, and was ribbing me all morning about having danced the 'Lambada' very erotically with Ana, but I am sure she exaggerates.

After lunch, the hour long walk to pick up the car cleared my head and I apologised to Ana, just in case. She said that I danced divinely and Andy called me a 'dirty old ficker'. I noticed that he modified the swearword in front of his wife, which lessened my indignation somewhat.

No weeding or grammar today.

Martes, 11 de Diciembre

Still feeling chastened over the barbecue; by myself, not by
Pamela, who is becoming quite tiresome by recalling new (to
me) incidents on an hourly basis. I refuse to believe that I
kissed Gary on the forehead. I have made use of my new
electric drill and put up the first of the curtain rails, in our
bedroom. Pamela hopes that it will keep the 'infernal cold' out
and I retorted by saying that cold can hardly be 'infernal'. She
said that I was grumpy and that it was the inevitable aftermath
of my 'excesses' on Sunday. I said I would begin to call her
'Pedantic Pamela' and laughed to prove that I was not grumpy.

One unenjoyable hour of pronouns to make up for
yesterday's lapse in my studies. I simply could not face the
subjunctive.

Miércoles, 12 de Diciembre

A cloudy day. Pamela put up the bedroom curtains and took
them down again. She says the rail is not straight. It looks
straight to me; perhaps the floor slopes. I have added a spirit
level to my Ferretería list and hope that my own spirits will
pick up today. Of all the golf club and other dinners which I
attended in my old life, I cannot recall ever 'letting my hair
down' to such an extent. Perhaps the change of country and
climate has lowered my inhibition threshold. I will drink far
less at the next social gathering that I attend. (Possibly
omit/modify the last four days from the published journal, lest

I give the future reader the impression that I am a dipsomaniac and thus lessen their respect for my other achievements.)

I put off my Ferretería visit until tomorrow and instead went for a restorative walk along the track leading south from the village. I was distressed to see four swimming pools in the first half mile and hurried past houses named 'Casa Harrison' and 'Finca O'Neil'. As a general rule I can see that Spanish house owners cultivate the land around them, while foreigners prefer stone chippings, a pool, and a few shrubs.

Jueves, 13 de Diciembre

A sunny day and I am also my old sunny self again. Pamela and I drove into town and I decided to accompany her to the supermarket before visiting the Ferretería, as the latter was so far the only place in Villeda that I had visited, apart from the Town Hall. I pushed the trolley and urged Pamela to buy Spanish food. She said that most foodstuffs were international in nature and that those that were 'typically Spanish' were the ones that I disliked. I said this was nonsense and told her to shop fearlessly. She placed in the trolley three different types of olives, garlic, cured ham, dried cod, soft (soggy, it turned out) cheese, anchovies, 'morcilla' sausage (black pudding without the stench), sundry other dried sausages, some huge prawns, and a large bottle of olive oil. I would, I said, scoff the lot. She also bought a lot of normal food and the bill was astronomical.

She insisted on accompanying me to the Ferretería, although I warned her that it was no place for women. She thought the 'queueing' protocol absurd and said that it appeared that I was not the only person who bought things for the sake of it. I found all my items except the pliers and, with Pamela hovering at my shoulder, decided not to request them today. I will return alone.

After a lunch of assorted dried meats, and toast on which Pamela spread a revolting paste known as 'sobreasada', I repaired to the rustic bar for coffee. Paco was there and we arranged our next class for tomorrow evening. He asked if we could translate 'You Are Always On My Mind'. I said, "Primero terminar 'To be' verbo," and he nodded; sadly, I thought.

Viernes, 14 de Diciembre

The colder weather has returned. I told Pamela that my Scandinavian thermal vests were very effective and she said that if she had wanted to wear thermal vests, she would have emigrated to Lapland. I lit the stove straight away and, an hour later, she went to see Laura. Such a waste of wood.

Paco arrived ten minutes late for the class, but I still gave him his full half hour, despite him looking meaningfully at his watch at half past seven. Paco grasped 'We are Paco and Ernest', but, when I pointed to myself and to the photograph of my Uncle Roger ('Bill' for our purposes) his understanding of 'You are Bill and Ernest' was shaky. Having only one word for 'you', as we do, should be a blessing, but it seemed to complicate matters. 'They are Bill and Susan' was introduced after half past and I saw that his heart was no longer in it, if it ever had been. In our final run-down of the verb, Paco could get no further than 'I am Paco, you are Ernest'. Very disappointing.

I kicked off my half hour of Spanish with, "Would you like to go to London?" to which Paco answered, "Sí." I asked him "Por qué?" (Why?) and he launched into a rapid monologue which I understood almost none of. Paco has little vocation as a teacher, or student, and I begin to despair.

Sábado, 15 de Diciembre

Sunny but cold, so I lit the stove. Two subjects have reared their heads today; one of them ugly, one less so. Pamela insists on having a television and also wants to begin our Christmas preparations. I plunged into the topic of Christmas to divert her attention from the television, but to no avail. It appears that she is getting 'hooked' on an after-lunch soap-opera which she watches at Laura's, and does not wish to intrude on her every single weekday. She once again extolled the virtues of televised listening comprehension and pointed out that there is no licence fee here, which brought me round somewhat. She promised that it would not be the thin edge of a satellite dish-shaped wedge and we agreed to purchase a set next week.

As for Christmas, I am all for following the Spanish traditions in this respect, but have as yet not ascertained what they are. I will consult the internet. Pamela absolutely insists on Turkey for Christmas Day, and I said that I was not sure that they bred them in Spain. She told me not to be stupid and that, in any case, with so many 'Brits' around they were bound to be available. I sadly agreed that this was more than likely to be the case. She has already ordered a box of crackers from Marks and Spencer.

Domingo, 16 de Diciembre

Cloudy and cold, so I lit the stove. The woodpile descends slowly but surely. According to the internet, the Spaniards' fondness for 'fiestas' of all kinds has led them to extend Christmas by another week. As far as I can see, they spend Christmas Eve ('Nochebuena' - 'Good Night') with their families and do absolutely nothing on Christmas Day, unless they go to church, of course, as some old people still do. New Year's Eve ('Nochevieja' - 'Old Night') is spent with friends (and family, I am sure) and they do much as we do, except that they eat as well as drink. At 12 o'clock they attempt to eat twelve grapes before the twelfth chime of the clock; curious and absurd. Not satisfied with these standard Christmas celebrations, they have also invented a 'Día de los Reyes Magos' ('Day of the Magical Kings'). These, I deduce, are the Three Kings, or Wise Men, who I thought had left Bethlehem by that date, but I may be mistaken. This day, the 6th of January, is also spent with family, and it is now that presents are distributed. All I can say is that, if I were a young boy hoping to receive a bicycle, I would be jolly annoyed to get it the day before I went back to school! I think they need to have a rethink regarding their holiday traditions.

Speaking of rethinking, I have once more rethought my exchange class strategy. This will be reported in the corresponding journal entry.

Lunes, 17 de Diciembre

Rather cold and windy, so I lit the stove. Pamela is adamant that a regulation Christmas Day will be celebrated, either in this house or elsewhere. She says that just the two of us here would be a dull affair, so she is going to ask Andy and Ana if they have anything planned. I said a nice, quiet, relations-free Christmas Day would be lovely and she burst into tears. Thankfully she soon stopped and said that she would miss our son, Gerald. As Gerald is in Australia living in a hippy commune, or 'agricultural cooperative' as he calls it, a Christmas get-together, I said, would be difficult to arrange. "I just want to be around *people* at Christmas," she said. Rather than point out that I was, in fact, a person, I said I would put my thinking cap on, and I have.

Of the four significant Christmas events, we are reliant on Andy for any Christmas Day festivity, as Spanish people appear to ignore the actual day of Christ's birth completely. I will, therefore, approach Paco regarding his scheduled movements on the other three dates, leaving Nora and Angeles as a last resort. This time next year, we will have so many Spanish friends that we will be parrying invitations from all sides, I am sure.

Martes, 18 de Diciembre

A cold, clear day. Stove lit. Pamela has complained about the cold when going to and getting up from bed. She said that my saying that I found it bracing did not wash and that, speaking of washing, the bathroom was also freezing cold. This resulted in our trip to the electrical shop in town yielding a flat-screen television set, an oil radiator and a fan heater. This has delivered a severe blow to our monthly budget even before the Christmas festivities have begun. Pamela says that we have plenty of money, but that is not the point. Our aim is to live unostentatiously and blend in with the humble villagers. She said that having a television and a couple of heaters is hardly akin to having a huge Mercedes on the driveway. We don't have a driveway, but I saw her point.

I connected the set and we can now watch all of the Spanish television channels, as well as several in the regional dialects. A few people in the Valencia region, within which we reside, are said to speak 'Valenciano', but I have yet to hear it spoken. Pamela says that they speak it here, but that I might not have noticed the difference. I am sure that I would have. In any case, I will stick to traditional 'Castellano' Spanish for at least a year before I dabble with Catalan, Basque etc., if it does turn out that people take these dialects seriously.

At least now I might see a little more of my wife, as today she stayed in to watch her after-lunch soap-opera. It consisted of a series of hysterical scenes on and around a ranch - a sort of 'Wild-Westenders'! Pamela said that it was a Columbian production. The Columbian accent may explain why I understood very little of it, although Pamela seemed to follow the rather passionate and overstated dialogue. I will find something more educational to watch when I wish to practise my listening comprehension.

Miércoles, 19 de Diciembre

It appears that I need not, until further notice, consult Pamela every single day about whether or not to light the stove. It *must* be lit, she says, every morning. It is rather irksome to clean out, rebuild and relight the fire every day, but Spanish peasants have been doing it for generations, or ever since the wood-burning stove was invented, and so shall I. Thermostat twiddling is no longer for me.

The beans and potatoes are coming along handsomely, aboveground at least, but I fear that my radish seeds were duds. Neither of us is over-fond of them, anyway. I hacked out the few weeds that I found with my trusty azada; much easier than bending down to pull them up.

Pamela drove over to see Andy and Ana, and it appears that we are to have Christmas dinner with many other 'Brits' at a German restaurant twenty miles away. I did not demur, for fear of more maternal tears, and will stoically see out the unwelcome event. On a lighter note, we are to spend New Year's Eve at their house, and most of the guests will be Ana's friends and family. This is good news! We are to have lunch on 'The Day of the Kings' with them too, as Laura and Paco are eating at her parents' house, and it is left to me to secure a dinner engagement for Christmas Eve. Unless I can make some very good friends very quickly, I fear I shall have to resort to Nora and Angeles.

Two hours spent preparing Paco's new, customised, syllabus.

Jueves, 20 de Diciembre

I popped into town to buy Pamela's Christmas presents and also purchased the pliers at the Ferretería. My list is now exhausted, so I browsed in vain. I considered buying a pair of overalls for my future D.I.Y. and horticultural tasks, but, conscious of our recent overspending, I will save them for next month. I later called in on Nora and Angeles and invited them to dinner on Christmas Eve. To my surprise, they accepted, and I feigned delight. This is short notice for Pamela to learn how to cook whatever they eat on Christmas Eve, but she did not complain, as the rest of the key meals will be given to us 'on a plate', so to speak.

Paco arrived with his Johnny Cash CD, as requested, and we set to translating the lyrics to 'Walk the Line', much to his delight and, I think, relief. I chose that song, from all the Country and Western song lyrics on the internet, as it only has four verses. I must confess that I decided upon this use of Paco's half hour as being of greatest *mutual* benefit; he would be happy, and I would have the extra linguistic challenge of translating the songs. The already-prepared translation of 'Walk the Line' took only ten minutes to impart, giving us time to sing the song, and correct Paco's pronunciation, five times. Pamela looked in during the fourth rendition to see if we were all right. For my half hour I suggested that we just chat, slowly, and that I would put my hand up each time I failed to understand something. I raised my hand many times during those thirty minutes and Paco is beginning to know what I do and do not understand. We toasted to our new strategy with our usual almond liqueur, after which, Paco gave me a rousing and partially comprehensible encore of 'Walk the Line'. He enjoys singing it even more, he says, now that he knows what it is about.

Today has been my most satisfactory day for a long time, and the oil radiator made preparing for bed and getting into it far more enjoyable.

Viernes, 21 de Diciembre

Light rain after eight dry days. I watched the news on television after lunch and understood most of it with the help of the pictures and graphs. The Spanish economy is booming and it appears that they expect half of Europe to retire here in the next few years, judging by the number of seaside and golfing resorts that are projected. I thought that Spain was short of water, but I must be mistaken. I considered the twenty minutes of sports (mostly football) news excessive, but enjoyed the extra-long weather forecast. They study each region in detail, which will help me to increase my geographical knowledge of my new country. We will take a trip in the spring and start to explore.

Half an hour of prepositions and half an hour of 'You Are Always On My Mind' lyrics.

Sábado, 22 de Diciembre

Sunshine and showers. Pamela went to do the shopping for our Christmas Eve dinner, which is to be a surprise, while I pottered about the house. I stuck some of the adhesive foam stripping on our bedroom windows, but had to remove it as the windows, being hermetic, would not then close. I had more success with the bedroom door, so I used the rest of it up on two and a half more doors. More foam stripping is on my new list. I surveyed my bare study and wondered where I could get suitable, inexpensive books quickly. A set of encyclopedias would look very well. I asked Pamela on her return, and she said that there are car-boot sales in villages nearer to the coast. "Run by the Spanish?" I asked. "Mixed," she replied. She then said that, if I was bored, I might like to sweep the upstairs of the house. I denied being bored, but said that I would be more than happy to sweep the upstairs, once she had finished sweeping the downstairs, which she was doing at the time. As a lifelong breadwinner, I sometimes forget that houses do not clean themselves.

Domingo, 23 de Diciembre

Sunny today. The onions have sprouted! Do vegetables always sprout in the night, or do I just fail to pay attention during the day? I mopped the upstairs of the house this morning without Pamela asking me to do so. She was grateful, but reminded me to change the water from time to time, and to put some cleaning liquid in it. I haven't mopped since I was in the Scouts and had forgotten these small details. I repositioned our bedroom curtain rail correctly with the help of the spirit level (the floor does not slope) and put up two more in the guest bedrooms. I felt that this was sufficient work for a Sunday and went to the rustic bar for a pre-lunch glass of beer with Paco.

It was the first time I had been to the bar at this time (1.00pm) on a Sunday and I was astonished at the number of men assembled. Everybody was talking loudly and the noise was overwhelming, as was the smoke. I appeared to be the only non-smoker present. Paco and I shouted at each other over our beer and he introduced me to two of his friends: Juan, a wizened old 'agricultor', and Pepe, a builder, plumber and electrician; he must have spent many years at college to become so multi-skilled. Old Juan only gaped at me and chomped the air, while Pepe addressed me in 'Indian Spanish', using the infinitive of verbs and gesticulating. A rough translation of his speech would be: 'You to live village, to like, very good, you to need swimming pool, I to build. Very cheap.' I found myself replying in the same manner: 'I to like village much, I not to need swimming pool. Not to like. If other work in house I to ring you.' This is a terrible habit which I must not get into. It is easier, it must be said, and it is understood, but if I speak this way they will take me for a foreigner or a congenital idiot forever.

At exactly two o'clock there was an exodus from the bar as the men went home for lunch. Many of these men would be in the bar again at half past three and I concluded that they made very little contribution to the housework. I don't feel that I can allow myself to integrate to such an extent, so after lunch I did the washing up, much to Pamela's surprise. From now on I will wash up after most meals.

Lunes, 24 de Diciembre, 'Nochebuena'

Early evening journal entry: Another crisp, sunny day. Most of the potatoes have now sprouted. Pamela has been cooking all afternoon and the kitchen has been out of bounds to me. The smells are most appealing. I received a very short email from Gerald wishing us a merry and 'eco-friendly' Christmas. I await the arrival of the mimic man and the chatterbox with trepidation.

Later journal entry: The dinner was an *unqualified* success. Pamela cooked the apparently traditional monk-fish with mushroom sauce, followed by leg of lamb with almonds and rice, to perfection. Nora and Angeles were rendered practically speechless during the meal, and I suspect that Angeles was overcome with astonishment at the quality of Pamela's exquisite cooking. She rallied and resumed her jabbering, but Pamela's Spanish is now so good that she is able to cut her off in mid-prattle and steer the conversation away from her blessed grandchildren onto more topical lines. Nora was also able to speak and even glanced at me occasionally as he did so. I spoke little, but thought long and hard before I did, which I believe has raised me in their linguistic estimations. Towards the end of the meal Nora looked me straight in the eye and said, "Feliz Navidad, Ernesto." We drank two bottles of good Rioja red and we all became quite jolly. Fortunately, Angeles does not drink alcohol, as her tongue is loose enough without it. They were amused by the crackers - Angeles yelped loudly on pulling hers - and Pamela told them the 'jokes', which did not translate well. We all wore our paper hats and took photos for posterity.

The dinner was so pleasant that I completely forgot about the ordeal which awaits me tomorrow.

Martes, 25 de Diciembre, Día de Navidad

A sunny Christmas Day! The first in my life that I can recall, although there must have been a few over the years. I wanted to defer present-giving until the traditional 'Day of the Kings', but Pamela was adamant that today we would follow *our* traditions. She gave me a Spanish travel book, a Spanish wine book, and a pair of overalls! I was delighted, especially with the books (the overalls less so, as they were on my new list), which I will read from cover to cover and will occupy a full three inches of shelf space. I gave Pamela two Spanish cookery books, a portable bread-making machine and some new oven mitts. She received the gifts graciously and added that there was a distinct 'kitchenesque' theme about them. I asked her not to dwell on the oven mitts, as they were a 'stocking filler', and that the bread machine was really a present to both of us, as I fully intended to do my share of the bread making. This pleased her, and she said that she was delighted with the books. So far so good.

The Teutonic Christmas dinner was the ordeal I had expected it to be and is thankfully now over. The fact that fourteen British and Irish people, and Ana, consented to be fed today of all days by Germans is beyond me. The war has been over for a long time, I know, but the fact that it prevented me from meeting my great-uncle Wilfred (killed at the battle of El Alamein, eleven years before my birth), the most interesting member of my family by far, still rankles. He was a young ventriloquist of great renown, and remained the major topic of conversation at family gatherings for several decades; but I digress.

Pamela buffered me from the Northern couple to our right, but the Scottish coast-dweller to my left was insufferable. The man, Robert by name, on finding that I had been a keen golfer, extolled the virtues of several golf courses, revelled in the pleasure of never having to play in the rain, and talked me through his new set of clubs and made-to-measure putter. He talked handicaps and bunkers, matchplay and chip shots, until I was for rushing to the course there and then. I *will not* play golf in Spain! The lunch was good, but seemed endless (I was driving), but Pamela seemed to enjoy talking to the Northerners, so my suffering was not altogether in vain. Andy drank too much and did an amusing Nazi walk, 'a la Basil Fawlty', when the staff were not present, which provided me with some light relief over coffee.

On the drive back, Pamela said that it was not a 'crime' to play golf, and that if I left the clubs in the boot of the car, none of the 'humble villagers' would know where I was going; not that they would care. If it stopped me from getting bored, she said, she was all for it. I brought my clubs to Spain with a view to selling them.

I will make some bread tomorrow.

Miércoles, 26 de Diciembre

Today is a normal working day, as the Spanish do not celebrate Boxing Day. Strange that they should omit a potential 'fiesta'. I investigated this, and the internet says that Boxing Day originated in the days when servants, after attending to their masters and mistresses on Christmas Day, were given the following day off to visit their families. They would often be given a box (sic) to take with them, which might contain gifts, some money, the leftovers of the Christmas dinner, or all three. In less enlightened, mostly Catholic, countries, the servants worked on the 26th too, which has left Spain's bereft of Boxing Day.

I bought some flour and yeast from the old hag in the windowless shop and set to my bread making. The machine only produces one loaf at a time and my first loaf failed to rise more than two inches and stuck stubbornly to the bottom, despite me following the instructions to the letter. I have chipped away the debris and left the recipient to soak. I will persevere.

One hour of reflexive pronouns, which are mostly unnecessary. In English, if I go, I go, but in Spanish I must say, 'I go myself.' This is preposterous as, if I am going somewhere, I will obviously take myself with me.

Jueves, 27 de Diciembre

Dreamt about golf - most disturbing. The cool, sunny weather continues and my plot looks lovely and weed-free, if a little bare. I wish I could plant more things, but it is not the time. I started to read my Spanish travel book with the help of the dictionary and finished the first two page; the acknowledgements. At this rate it will take me between four and five months to finish it. I may order the English version of the book to speed my progress, as I am anxious to increase my knowledge of my new country. I shall not read the wine book from cover to cover, but rather dip into it and discover new wines to purchase. I may lay down a cellar, in the pantry.

One hour studying negatives in Spanish. Unlike English, the Spanish language cannot get enough of double negatives, and saying 'I don't want nothing' is considered correct. This will take some getting used to, after all the ear-boxing I suffered for saying such things at my preparatory school. Pamela says that I should be aware that Spanish is a different language and not just a 'code' for English. I think I know what she means by this, but I am not sure.

Viernes, 28 de Diciembre

A misty morning - most unusual. We must, I have decided, have a name for the house, and it will *not* be Casa Postlethwaite! I will think of imaginative names and have asked Pamela to do the same. On the spur of the moment I suggested 'Casa Destino', but Pamela vetoed that, saying it sounded utterly ridiculous. I will look for suitable names on the internet.

Pamela has made a loaf with the bread-making machine and it has turned out perfectly. What was the secret? The secret was, she said, to follow the instructions, stir the mixture well, and not to hurry. She has a gift for cookery which I may not possess.

Another successful exchange class with Paco, although almost all the exchange of knowledge now passes from me to him. This serves our purposes well, as I, after all, need to master my adopted language and Paco merely wishes to understand his warblings. I imparted my translation of 'You Are Always On My Mind', we sang it three times, and we then talked in Spanish about the different regions of Spain. I learnt that the Catalans are tight-fisted, the Galician people sneaky, the Andalucians lazy, the Basques hot-headed, and the 'Valencianos', especially 'Alicantinos', are wonderful. This is Paco's opinion, not mine, and I detect a hint of bias and over-generalisation. When I travel, I will see for myself.

Sábado, 29 de Diciembre

Overcast and chilly. The woodpile descends markedly. I suggested 'Casa Progreso' as a house name and Pamela said that that would be setting the high-jump bar very high. I said that I had not heard that remarkable expression before, and she realised that it was a Spanish one that she had unwittingly translated. She thinks in Spanish a lot these days, she says, and will be dreaming in it next! I am not jealous, merely slightly envious, of her linguistic progress. I tried to think in Spanish for an hour this afternoon, but only managed ten very restricting minutes.

I took coffee in the clean bar and am beginning to understand a little more of the waitress's chatter. I wish I could put my hand up as I do with Paco, but she might think it odd. I saw in the regional newspaper that a new golf course is due to open only fifteen miles from here. I will write an advertisement for my golf clubs on the computer before I am led into temptation.

Domingo, 30 de Diciembre

Sunny but fresh. I watched the news on television this morning and will do so every day from now on. This will get the old brain ticking away in Spanish for the rest of the day. I am determined to start thinking in it before Pamela begins to dream in it. Pamela doesn't always remember her dreams, so she may have already started without realising.

After lunch, and washing up once more, I pottered about in my study talking Spanish to myself. I told the absent listener where I was from, where I lived, what I liked and disliked, where I would like to go, and also gave him or her a long list of items that you can buy at the Ferretería. It was not a long monologue, but two months ago it would have lasted for less than half a minute, so I *have* made a lot of progress. As Pamela said, when she came to see who I was talking to, one should rejoice in what one knows, rather than despair at what one does not know. Good advice, and in no way delivered in a condescending way, from my lovely wife.

Lunes, 31 de Diciembre,'Nochevieja'

A sunny end to the year! This time last year I was stuck indoors waiting to go to yet another golf club dinner, which Pamela, it turns out, found even more tiresome than I did. It has been an excellent year for Spain too, according to the news, as the property market continues to flourish and everybody is better off. I hope Spain does not become too advanced, as I like it just the way it is.

I went to the big supermarket in town to buy some Spanish

champagne, known as 'cava', for tonight's bash. It was quite cheap and I fear it cannot be very good at that price. I also intended to buy some more Spanish food, but we have yet to eat most of what we bought on our last visit. Pamela has said that, as with golf, it is not a 'crime' to dislike certain foods. I retorted that when we eat out, communal salads will always be liberally dashed with olive oil and vinegar, instead of tasteful salad dressing. I suppose she is right, though, in that I should not have to torture myself by eating raw meats if I do not wish to.

I will report on tonight's dinner in tomorrow's journal entry, as I will be too fatigued when we return.

Martes, 1 de ENERO, 2008, 'El día del año nuevo'

Feliz año nuevo, journal! Last night's dinner was splendid; far more enjoyable than the foreigners' barbecue and far more civilised. Spanish people know how to enjoy themselves without drinking excessively, which is just as well, as they all drove home afterwards. I am sure there are breathalyser tests here too, but perhaps the police were seeing in the New Year as well.

We were eleven to dinner and Andy was the only foreigner apart from ourselves. Ana's parents were present, as well as assorted uncles, aunts and cousins, including Beatríz, the deaf one, who was seated at my side. This did not curtail my participation in the conversation; indeed, the fact that everyone spoke at the same time made it almost irrelevant who your neighbours were. This random conversational exchange suited me, as I could chip in whenever I was able to, and rely on Pamela to 'put my comments into context', as she calls it.

The food was delicious. There were so many small dishes to choose from that I was easily able to avoid the cured ham, and our dozen 'twelve o'clock grapes' each came in individual tins. They were seedless and I had no difficulty in eating them before the twelfth chime, unlike old Tío (Uncle) Arsenio, who almost choked. When he had recovered, I asked him if he was related to the founder of the village. Andy translated his reply as, "No, they think the second Viscount shagged one of my ancestors, a scullery maid, and the name has stuck." The 'cava' was excellent and far better value for money than French champagne, although being required to eat 'turrón' with it, a nougat and nut sweet which was as hard as nails and just as inedible, confused the palate somewhat.

A man of fifty-four does not normally make New Year Resolutions, as he is usually set in his ways, but my new life requires new challenges! I resolve to:

Speak Spanish well before the year is out.
Become an accomplished horticulturist.
Become an accomplished handyman.
Do my share of the housework, except cookery.
Start to get to know my new country.
Not play golf.

I will review my progress in one year's time. An additional resolution will be to avoid my journal turning into a mere diary. In order to achieve this, I will no longer oblige myself to write every single day, but make meaningful, well-considered entries as I see fit. The future reader, I feel sure, will not wish to hear about every mundane task that I carry out, although I believe that I have successfully avoided pedantry and repetition up to now. It has certainly been an action-packed two months!

Miércoles, 2 de Enero

Cloudy and cold. My daily journal entry is going to be a hard habit to kick! Speaking of habits, the dope fiend next door made his first appearance, to my knowledge, on his 'plot' for a while, and this time with his wife, or partner, who I had never seen before. She is even swarthier than him; almost coloured, in fact, and going to fat. They must be in their early thirties, although it is hard to tell, and don't appear to have any children. I expect his drug use has rendered him impotent. I waved politely and she said, "Hola, muchacho." They were pacing around the rusty cars, so hopefully they are planning to have them removed in the near future. I looked up 'muchacho' and it means 'boy'. Either my healthy lifestyle has rejuvenated me, or she is very impudent, or both. One hour of conditionals after weeding.

Additional journal entry:

On mentioning my encounter with the neighbours to Pamela on her return from town, she said that gypsies used the words 'muchacho' and 'muchacha' as a term of endearment. Gypsies! I did not know that they were gypsies. Pamela said that she knew from the moment we moved in and, as I had not realised and immediately 'passed judgement', thought it better not to raise the matter. I replied that I am not a racialist and do not 'pass judgement', and she laughed. The gypsy lady, it turns out - for Pamela knows everything - is an accomplished singer and he accompanies her on the guitar. We see them so seldom, she says, because they are often travelling to 'gigs', by which she means concerts.

So the right-hand neighbours, having momentarily gone down in my estimations for being gypsies, have now risen again due to being accomplished. I admire accomplishment of any description, not being excessively accomplished myself, yet.

Jueves, 3 de Enero

Cold, but warm in the sun. I asked Pamela if she thought that our neighbours would allow us to go to see them perform and she said that, as far as she knew, their concerts were open to members of the public, even gypsy-haters. I laughed at her little joke and said that I would call round to ask them when their next local concert was to take place. She doubted that they would play in a town as small as Villeda, but that she too would like to see them perform. I will prepare my questions before I call round.

Today's class was as enjoyable as the last. We studied and performed 'Folsom Prison Blues' and then talked about music in general. Paco said that my neighbours were quite well-known in the world of 'Flamenco' and I asked him, if this was the case, why they had rusting cars on their plot. He said, I think, that they lived for their 'Art' and didn't pay attention to such mundane things. I wish they would. He is not averse to coming to see them in concert, if Pamela and I wish to go, but considers Flamenco music a very poor relation to Country and Western. I didn't know the two styles were related, but I think I know what he was trying to say, although I am not sure. Gypsies are known as 'gitanos' and lady gypsies, 'gitanas' (throat clearing on the initial 'g').

Sábado, 5 de Enero

Colder today. Pamela insisted on leaving the radiator on all night and I shudder to think what the electricity bill will amount to. Better than shuddering with cold, I suppose. At least it didn't freeze my plot and I'm sure that the winter will soon be over. I still favour the name 'Casa Progreso' for the house and, as Pamela has not actually vetoed it, it remains my first choice at the moment. I asked her for suggestions, but she says she prefers the discreet '2' that it currently sports.

We watched an interesting documentary about the fauna of Africa last night. I was getting the gist of the commentary; not difficult when stalking, pouncing and devouring lions put things nicely into context, when Pamela started prodding the remote control and David Attenborough took over proceedings. This facility is known as 'Dual' and allows you to watch programmes in the original language. Pamela was delighted, as she likes David Attenborough, and we suffered his annoying tones for the last twenty minutes of the programme. I felt like I was back on Swinburne Crescent and fear that this discovery may diminish our future listening comprehension opportunities.

I am so looking forward to tomorrow's 'Lunch of the Kings'!

Domingo, 6 de Enero

The fourth and final event of the Christmas calendar, the 'Day of the Kings' lunch, has been the most memorable. The New Year's Eve guests were all present, as well as a smattering of young children and a teenage boy. We made Ana and Andy a present of a dozen bottles of cava; a half dozen to be consumed *in situ* and a rather superior half dozen for them to enjoy at their leisure. Andy said that I was going to make him even more of a drunken fecker than he already was. I suppose his variations around the swearword are better than him saying the word itself, but he will soon run out of vowels.

Other presents were conspicuous by their absence. The children, it seems, had received almost all of their presents on Christmas Day, in order to enjoy them during the holidays. This is not what the internet said, and I fear that Anglo-American practices are creeping in here too. The teenage boy, whose name I don't recall, had apparently been 'glued to his X-box' for the duration of the holiday and had not done his homework. Modernity may not suit the Spanish youth.

The lunch consisted of many small dishes, some of which I partook and some of which I did not. I avoided the octopus, the dried blood (sic) and the dried cod with very greasy peppers, but gorged myself on the mushrooms filled with bacon, cheese and cream, later asking Ana to give Pamela the recipe. The taste of the post-lunch cava was spoilt for me once again by having to eat a ring-shaped pastry known as 'Roscón de Reyes', and more of that scarcely edible 'Turrón'. Uncle Arsenio's teeth becoming embedded in a piece of the monstrous stuff, and his subsequent removal and waving about of them, caused much merry laughter. I would have preferred a little cheese with my cava, if anything.

It was at this point that Andy announced that Ana was expecting a child. This was indeed good news, but the uproar that ensued was, I felt, a little overstated. There was much screeching, yelping and kissing from the ladies and bellowing and hugging from the men, while the children ran round and round the table screeching, "Bebé, bebé!" Uncle Arsenio grabbed and shook Andy's genitals and said, "Muchacho potente!" several times, before being taken for a lie down. The Spanish really are exceedingly fond of children! When we found that Pamela was expecting Gerald, we spent the evening deciding if we could afford for her to give up her part-time job at the library for more than a few months.

All in all, a splendid day, and the fact that I have written this journal entry today and not tomorrow is thanks to my moderate consumption of the cava and preceding wines. I shall not become a 'drink-driver', even though it is very much the tradition here.

Lunes, 7 de Enero

Cloudy and less cold. I must confess that I am rather glad that all the seasonal festivities are over for this year. It has been an interesting and mostly enjoyable time, but I am not much of a 'party animal' and much prefer the steady, day to day routine of the 'student of life'.

Armed with my questions, in my head and my shirt pocket, I called on our musical neighbours this morning. They didn't answer the door, so I called again after lunch. He looked sleepy and I imagine that they may have returned late from a performance last night. I formally introduced myself as his new next-door neighbour and he gave me a peculiar, befuddled look, perhaps considering our casual greeting across the plots to be sufficient introduction. He is called Pedro and his wife, for she is in fact his wife, is called Rocío ('Rothío'). She called from the other room, "Quién coño está allí?" ('Who [unknown word] is there?') 'Coño', I later discovered, is a very vulgar word indeed and not one that ladies ought to use. I only report the word here as a warning to future readers who may be learning Spanish. In spite of her foul language, she was very welcoming and offered me a can of beer. Although early in the day for me (4.17pm), I felt it would have been impolite to refuse, so I accepted it and, no glass being offered, sipped from the actual can itself. I told them that I was very interested in Flamenco music - not strictly true, yet - and asked them when they would be performing nearby. She spoke very quickly indeed in a very lispy voice and, of her lengthy torrent of speech, I only understood, 'Alicante', 'Sábado', 'muchacho', 'hijo' (son) and 'niño'. Perhaps she thinks me childlike because I don't speak Spanish very well. Pedro, seeing my confusion, took my pen and paper and wrote the name of the concert venue and the time and date. I gave them the 'thumbs up' sign, something I never did until I came to Spain, and said goodbye.

On returning home smelling of beer, Pamela joked - unamusingly, I thought - that my boredom was driving me to drink, but we agreed to drive down to Alicante on Saturday to see them 'do their stuff'. I look forward to it and to expanding my rapidly expanding cultural knowledge. I expect that we will be the only non-gypsies present.

Miércoles, 9 de Enero

The mild weather continues. In the last two days I have resumed my industrious and studious lifestyle with gusto. I have taken no wine, walked vigorously in the countryside twice, studied my grammar, and put up four more curtain rails. Pamela, hot on my heels, has put up the curtains and they do look splendid. Ana and Laura also have some curtains, so we are not the only people in the country to use them.

At last we have received an email of more than one sentence

from Gerald. I maintain that the convenience of modern technology is no excuse for neglecting the art of letter-writing, and he has finally 'come up with the goods'. He writes that his 'Agricultural Cooperative' is flourishing and that they have installed more solar panels. They have set up a school for the children - not his, I trust - to avoid the 'noxious influence of capitalist education', and are digging a new well. They are eschewing 'the scourge of money', he says, as much as possible, and he is very happy. He would like to come to visit us in the spring, but says that he lacks the means, and hates to think of the pollution that all those 'air miles' would cause.

Pamela insists on sending him the 'means' to buy his ticket and says that the other five hundred passengers on the plane can take the blame for the 'air miles'. She hasn't seen him for two years, and nor have I, and would very much like to. I suppose that paying his airfare is better than incurring the horrendous expense of our flights to Australia, a hire car, and the hotel bill, as I would *not* be prepared to sleep in a teepee on a hippie commune.

Half an hour of indefinite articles and half an hour of 'Your Cheatin' Heart'.

Jueves, 10 de Enero

So mild that Pamela said I needn't light the stove this morning! The woodpile is down to the last three layers of logs and I trust it will be enough to see the winter out. Pamela went into town to shop and to transfer rather a lot of 'means' to Gerald, so I see that he is not so averse to money as to dispense with his bank account. I am, nonetheless, looking forward to seeing him. He will no longer be able to criticize my 'materialistic existence', my 'slave-driven drudgery' and my 'golf club hobnobbing'. Instead he will see a man as close to the land as himself, leading a simple life and heating his home with an ecological wood-burning stove. As far as I am aware, he knows no Spanish, so he may also be impressed by my relative mastery of the language.

A sombre class today. Paco was so moved by the (actual meaning of) the words to 'Your Cheatin' Heart' that he spent the Spanish section of the class sobbing between replies to my questions about Spanish gypsy culture. He said that Flamenco music could be very moving, but couldn't touch Hank Williams at his best. He and Laura are unable to accompany us to the concert on Saturday as they have to go to see an ailing aunt in Almansa. This may or may not be an excuse; I will question him about the visit and his aunt's health in our next class.

The beans, potatoes and onions are flourishing, but the garlic appears to be dormant. Nor are the plum, cherry and pear trees exerting themselves to any visible degree. Never mind; spring will soon be upon us!

Sábado, 12 de Enero

It has only been necessary to light the stove in the evenings for the last two days, at the negligible expense of two medium and two large logs. Andy and Ana are unable to accompany us to the concert due to her 'condition'. Andy says that the excitement and strong emotions of Flamenco music might be too much for her. I am sure that he was struggling to suppress a smile when he said this, but I cannot be sure. She is only about two months 'gone'. He advised us to dress down a little and that Pamela ought not to take a handbag. He did not fear for our safety, he said, in the 'tablao' itself, but said that that Alicante was, "a shit-hole full of thieving bastards." I can't believe this, and the internet certainly paints a very different picture, but I shall wear my plastic digital watch and use my handy leg wallet just in case. I will report on tonight's adventure tomorrow, as we may arrive home quite late. Pamela did suggest us staying in a hotel and taking a taxi to the 'tablao', but I consider that an unnecessary expense. Alicante is only one hour away by car and I have printed out a street-plan of the area.

Domingo, 13 de Enero

The last twenty-four hours have been the most eventful of my time in Spain and, it must be said, among the most eventful of my life. I will use a narrative form to take future readers through my experiences in the same order in which they happened.

The drive to, and arrival in, Alicante was fairly straightforward. I reached the part of the city where I knew the 'tablao' to be without a hitch, but then drove round endlessly - and apparently aimlessly, Pamela said - looking for a place to park. I saw no reason to use an expensive car park and, after only half an hour of touring the district, I found a space. Pamela feared that we were going to be late, but she needn't have worried as, when we finally found the 'tablao' and went inside, we were the only customers apart from a brightly dressed young lady who Pamela said was probably a whore. (I disagreed, but later had to admit that she may have been right.) We had arrived twenty minutes after the advertised commencement and, on Pamela asking, were told that the first performance would get under way within the hour. Very Español, I must say! I unstrapped my leg wallet from my calf in the bathroom, put my actual wallet in my inside pocket, and stored the leg wallet in another pocket. It seemed like an unnecessary precaution, as Alicante did not look at all like Andy had described it.

Patrons filtered in, and amongst them there were very few of the gypsy hue. From overhearing the subsequent conversations, as there was as yet no music, we determined that they were from Germany, Holland, France or Belgium, indeterminate Nordic countries, Ireland, every part of the British Isles, and Spain - although the table of Spanish speakers may have been Argentinian, Pamela said. This was disappointing, but I think the lady of possibly ill repute was Spanish, and the waiters.

When I was just beginning to feel sleepy, the first performance began; an old gypsy man with his guitar. He looked very frail and he started to play very slowly, but soon speeded up and his gnarled fingers moved up and down the guitar neck like those of a much younger man. I think he was very good, but I can't be sure. When he slowed down again, one of the foreigners 'oléd' and the man gave him a withering look and bared his gums. He speeded up and slowed down several more times, stopped suddenly, bowed briefly, and hobbled off the stage. He spent the rest of the evening at the bar drinking a pale wine and smoking, and did not once look at the stage. Did he feel that playing to foreigners was 'beneath him'? I suspect so.

Next it was the turn of some 'gitana' dancers, accompanied on the guitar by two swarthy youths. 'Oléing', it appeared, was now permissible and the foreigners did so to excess, none more than a table of uncouth northerners who were drinking far too much beer, out of pint glasses, and behaving as if they were in a working men's club. Shouting, "Olé, f**cking olé," as one fat man in a football top did, was beyond the pale. I don't think the dancers were very good, but I can't be sure.

What I can be sure of is that Rocío and Pedro, who are *our neighbours*, were marvellous. Just as the dancers finished, some well-dressed Spanish people began to drift in, several apparent 'gitanos' amongst them. They helped to inspire a great hush in the room and caused the table of riff-raff to leave, the fat man saying, "f**ck this for a game of soldiers," as he left. (I report this reluctantly, in order to give the future reader the full picture of the soon to be sublime evening.)

My neighbours took to the stage to subdued clapping and restrained, anticipatory 'olés'. Pedro, seated on a stool, began to play slowly and beautifully, making me think that the toothless old man was not as good as I had thought. He had us spellbound, while Rocío walked round the stage looking intense and carrying her weight very gracefully indeed. Then she erupted into song. Bearing in mind that there were no microphones, the fact that her heart-rending wails filled the large 'tablao' is proof enough of the tremendous power of her voice. (Paco says that Johnny Cash had an incredibly powerful voice - I wish he could have been here, Paco I mean, because Johnny Cash would probably have joined in.) But volume alone does not moveth man, or woman. The passion, the beauty, the *realness* of her singing was truly astonishing. I had almost forgotten that Pedro was there, but he *was* there, playing sublimely.

I was captivated, and the hour during which she sang seemed like an eternity, or a very short time, depending on which way you looked at it. My heart was full, and fuller still when, after the last guitar note sounded and they descended from the stage to rapturous applause, they made straight for our table! How I wished I had brought my camera, which I had left behind due to Andy's warnings. They had a drink with us and I found it difficult to articulate my feelings, so Pamela helped me, and, when Rocío planted a crimson kiss on my right cheek, I couldn't have been happier.

I was less happy half an hour later when we discovered that our car had been stolen. At first I wasn't sure that we were on the same street, but Pamela, ever observant, said that the tobacconist's shop next to which we had parked was unlikely to have moved or cloned itself. She can be very bitter when the chips are down. I took out my mobile phone to ring the insurance company, but realised that the number was in the car. Pamela hailed a taxi, talked rapidly to the driver, and we soon arrived at the police station. She told the taxi driver, and me, to wait, reappeared ten minutes later, and talked even more rapidly to the driver, who responded succinctly and apparently correctly. During this time I felt myself invisible. It was only when I closed the hotel room door behind us that she spoke to me, calling me a 'bloody fool', and saying that I was 'tighter than a duck's arse', for not having used a car park. When Pamela is in one of those irrational moods it is best to 'bite the bullet' and keep quiet.

Today, after another visit to the police station and a call to the insurance company, we arrived home by taxi, courtesy of said insurance company, two hours ago. As Pamela told me to, "go and write all that in your damn diary," I decided to do so right away, and have written the above lengthy *journal* entry, in which I hope the unfortunate car incident does not overshadow my rather good, I think, description of the marvellous discovery of the talent and fame of our eminent neighbours. Pamela seems to have forgotten all about that, but one sometimes remembers the positive moments in one's life at a later date.

Lunes, 14 de Enero

Colder and overcast. Pamela has been very quiet all day today. I suspect that she feels remorseful about her overreaction to the loss of the car, although she may still be simmering. I pointed out over breakfast that ours wasn't the only car on that street, although it may have been the newest, and that the insurance company might give us an even newer one if it doesn't turn up. She just said, "fat chance," practically her only words to me this morning.

I took the bus into town to collect the car that the insurance company have provided us with while we wait to see if our car turns up. I rather hope it doesn't, as it would be a constant reminder to Pamela of the unfortunate incident. The insurance company man thinks it will probably be en route to Albania by now, where many cars find their way, he says, from the civilised half of Europe.

I called in at the Ferretería to ask about bookshelves. Shuffle as I would at the counter, I could not avoid being attended by the first and blankest of the blank-faced assistant, who either doesn't like me, or his job, or both. His insolence was such that I will reproduce our conversation, translated into English, in its entirety:

"Good morning. I need some bookshelves."

"This is a Ferretería."

"I know. Do you have bookshelves?"

"Man, this is a Ferretería."

"I believe Ferreterías sell most things."

"Man, we don't sell eggs, bread or fish."

"They are foods."

"Man, we don't sell newspapers, guitars or microwave ovens."

"Where can I buy bookshelves?"

"At the carpenter's, where they deal in wood."

"Thank you. Goodbye."

"Goodbye."

I am not sure if repeatedly calling me 'man' ('hombre') exacerbates his insolence, but I will find out. I may report him to his manager, when I discover which of the assistants is in fact the manager.

I asked for and received directions to a 'carpentería', and there explained my requirements over the noise of a blaring radio. How the four men there can work, day in and day out, to the sound of pop music and constant commercials, I do not know. A little classical music would be more soothing, I am sure. I was quoted an extremely high price by an extremely short man and asked him if there was not a cheaper alternative. He shrugged and said, "planks of wood." Of course! I had forgotten that I am now a budding DIY enthusiast. The short man showed me some nice planks and I ordered them to be cut to the correct length. I shall have to buy brackets, more screws and plugs, sandpaper and wood varnish! I paid for the wood and realised that they would not fit in the little Japanese car that the insurance company has lent us. Our new car, or returned car, when we get one or the other, shall have a roof-rack as befits all serious handymen. I telephoned Andy and he agreed to come to town in his van within the hour. He is a good friend and is never too busy to help, although I still sometimes think of him as a Scotsman rather than as a person. (Clarify or omit.)

Andy arrived as promised and we loaded the van before going to a bar for a drink. He wanted to know all about the concert and I described to him in great detail the beauty and passion of our neighbours' performance, only adding as a brief after-note the theft of the car. He was, as I had feared, more interested in the theft of the car and Pamela's reaction to it than the concert itself.

"So you're in the fecking doghouse, then!" he said with much glee. He added that he and Ana also had their occasional 'tiffs' and that buying her a gift normally did the trick. I said that I wasn't sure that Pamela would be so easily appeased, but Andy said that he knew women like the back of his foreskin, which failed to shock me, and that she would. When we had finished our small glass of beer and tasty 'tapa' of 'patatas bravas' ('brave potatoes?'), he took me to a trinket shop and chose a bracelet for me to give to Pamela. It wasn't expensive, but he said that it would suffice for the severity of my 'crime'. He had, he said, only had to buy Ana unscheduled gifts of gold on two occasions. I didn't ask him why.

Well, it turned out that Andy was right. Pamela liked the bracelet, put it on, and gave me a peck on the cheek. I said that it wasn't expensive and she replied that it was the thought that counted. Andy's thought, I thought, but didn't say. At fifty-four my knowledge of the female species is not yet complete.

Miércoles, 16 de Enero

The main news of the last two days has been the COLD. Temperatures plummeted on Monday night and have not risen above seven degrees since. Last night the thermometer registered SIX DEGREES BELOW ZERO and the oil radiator *and* the fan heater were on at full pelt all night. I fear for my crops, but my main concern right now is firewood. The woodpile has descended at an alarming rate and the wood-man says he will replenish our stock as soon as he can, but that he is very busy. He said (to Pamela - my telephone Spanish is still mediocre) that all the 'new foreigners' had run out of wood and that he was rushed off his feet. Pamela says that she will go to stay at Laura's or Ana's if the wood runs out, and I wish to avoid this at all costs. If a man cannot keep his wife warm, he is not much of a man.

I drove out to some nearby woods to forage for firewood and found seven sticks that will last about an hour at the present rate of combustion.

Jueves, 17 de Enero

Last night the thermometer registered NINE DEGREES BELOW ZERO and the water was frozen until midday. It is very sunny, but this is little consolation to Pamela, who has begun to pack a small travel bag. The wood-man has not answered his phone all day; very ominous. We are down to the last layer of logs and I fear for my new planks/shelves. Pamela said that, "wood is wood," but me suggesting, rather facetiously, that we start burning the furniture did not go down well. I can, I said, hardly be held responsible for the weather, but Pamela replied that I *am* responsible for having chosen a place to live at six-hundred metres above sea-level. I foresee another visit to the trinket shop when the cold snap is over.

Pamela spent the rest of the day at Laura's, so Paco and I were able to have our class in the living room. We plodded through the song 'Sixteen Tons', which made me think of coal, and I then asked Paco meteorological questions. He said that there were always very cold spells in winter here, and that it sometimes snowed. Snow! The estate agency website neglects to feature this in their photos, in which it is always summer. Nor do they mention that the record high and low temperatures are of 46 degrees Celsius and MINUS 18 DEGREES CELCIUS! Paco proudly stated that the area enjoys one of the widest temperature ranges in the whole of Europe and that this is why most foreigners prefer to live nearer to the coast. I shall not relay this information to Pamela.

Sábado, 19 de Enero

Last night the thermometer registered five degrees below zero. I had brought down the first plank and was about to go to ask Nora for the loan of a saw (now on my list, along with an axe) when the wood-man arrived! Fate has destined that I *shall* make the shelves! The price of the wood has gone up by 10%

and the wood-man astonished me by saying, "supply and demand," in English. I wonder where he has learnt that convenient phrase?

I soon got the stove roaring for all it was worth, while Pamela unpacked her bag. I am saved from the embarrassment of my wife evacuating herself. After a flying visit to the Ferretería, I put up the final curtain rails and turned my attention to the planks. They are already very smooth and only needed a cursory sandpapering. I then varnished one side of two of them on the study floor, before my hands became too cold to hold the brush. Some heating will need to be arranged for my study too, although the oil radiator does have little wheels.

One hour of grammar revision and another David Attenborough documentary - half in Spanish and half in slow, pedantic English. I admire the man's work, but one tires of his voice.

Domingo, 20 de Enero

Just below freezing point last night, but Pamela dropped a bombshell this morning that froze me more than the weather. On Tuesday she is going to go Line Dancing! I asked her if Line Dancing was popular in Spain, and she replied that as far as she knew it was not. It appears that a group of mainly foreign people, mostly women, meet at the 'Casa de Cultura' in Villeda once a week to practise under the instruction of Ernie, a Yorkshireman and Line Dancing 'maestro'. Pamela says that with Laura, Ana, other villagers to whom she chats, and the television, she gets all the Spanish practice that she needs, and that it would be rather nice to speak English from time to time. I pointed out that our language of communication, at least for the time being, was English. She replied that she wanted to chat with other women, in English, and talk about all the things she has talked about for the last fifty years. She did not, she said, intend to cut herself off from her past by 'going native' and that, although it seemed to be my intention, it had never been hers.

Bearing in mind the recent car theft fiasco, I chose diplomacy over persuasion, but I am as determined as ever not to drift into an expat lifestyle. To emphasise this resolve to myself, and to make a subtle point to Pamela, I wrote an advertisement for my set of excellent golf clubs on the computer, in Spanish and English. I have printed a dozen copies and will place them in appropriate locations. I shall also give some copies to Pamela for her to show to the Line Dancers, whose husbands will have more use for them than myself. In all likelihood, the buyer of the clubs will be an expat and this will prove once and for all that I am not one of them!

TWO hours of assorted grammar and one hour trying to follow a Spanish film. My brain was tired after the grammar and Pamela had to explain what was happening. I did pick out the word 'coño' several times, but Pamela says that it is not nearly so vulgar as our version of the word. This is a relief, as the great 'Diva' next door uses the word very freely.

Martes, 22 de Enero

The weather has returned to 'normal' cold. Alas, the beans appear to have perished. The internet says that they don't withstand extreme cold very well and surely Nora must have known this, having lived here all his life. Nor did Andy dismiss the beans as a mistake. I will quiz him, as I find communication with Nora so difficult; his mimes lack the profundity of words.

Pamela enjoyed her first Line Dancing session. She said that it was good exercise and that she had met some nice women and had a good chat over coffee afterwards. Ernie, she says, is incredibly sprightly for a seventy-four year old. He was the only man present, which is good news. She gave out some copies of my advertisement and the ladies expressed surprise at me forsaking the game in such an ideal place. "I told them you had bad knees," she said. I asked her why she had told this lie and she replied that it was better than saying I was a snob, an Anglophobe, or just weird.

I varnished most of the planks this morning, before deciding where to put the first one. I put up two brackets and placed a shelf upon them. I was pondering how to stop the books falling off the sides when Pamela brought me a cup of tea. She pondered alongside me for a moment and then pointed out that the brackets of the higher shelf would serve as bookends for the lower. Brilliant! That would, however, leave the very top shelf 'bookendless' and she suggested that I use it for my future collection of Flamenco CDs, which reminds me that I must pay our illustrious neighbours a visit.

One hour of mixed tenses, before watching half a football match. I don't like football, but may need the vocabulary, as

Spanish men are overly fond of the game; watching it in the bar, that is.

Miércoles, 23 de Enero

I called on Rocío and Pedro yesterday afternoon and they were watching the same soap-opera that Pamela watches. Great artists also need to relax, I suppose. Pedro's eyes were very red and there was a herbaceous smell in the room. Another form of relaxation, no doubt, but I must not judge a great artist as I am not one of them. I told them once again how much I had enjoyed the concert and Rocío said, "Coño, eso no era nada" ('[hard to define word], that was nothing.'). She explained, nice and slowly today, that they did 'guiri' (pronounced 'giri') concerts from time to time, but that they normally took it much more seriously. I asked them where I would be able to purchase one of their CDs and Pedro took one out of a drawer by his side and tossed it into my lap. I offered to pay for it and he said, "No, no," which were the only words he said during my visit. I asked them to sign it, which they did; 'Para Ernesto', and Rocío said she had noticed that we had a different car. I had not wanted to mention the loss of our car, but now that I had to, I did not make a fuss about it, as I know that great artists are above such mundane matters. As I expected, she did not seem surprised and said that it would probably be in Albania by now.

On returning home, I found that 'guiri' is a disrespectful term for foreigners. Perhaps we will go to a 'non-guiri' concert of theirs one day and set ourselves apart from the 'guiri' hoards. I suppose I will always be a 'guiri' in some people's eyes, but

88

never an expat.

Half an hour spent looking for disrespectful Spanish words on the internet - there are an awful lot - and half an hour translating 'King of the Road'. (I should point out to the future reader that my song translations for Paco are only approximate and that I guess the English words that I do not understand, such as 'stogie'. It would be dishonest not to tell them.) (I should also point out that I did not look up swearword for my own use, but in order to recognise them when they are spoken to me, about me, or at me.)

Viernes, 25 de Enero

Yesterday I put all eight shelves up; four on one wall and four on another, and they look wonderful, if a little empty. I have calculated that I will need about 250 books to fill the six lower shelves and must start to locate some. Pamela says she will ask about markets and car boot sales at her next Line Dancing session. Ideally, I would like half to be in Spanish and half in English, and a set of encyclopedias in each language would be a good start. I must also start to think about some furniture for the room, but I am having doubts about buying an extensive collection of Flamenco music. I have listened to Rocío and Pedro's CD three times now and, try as I may, I cannot enjoy it as much as I did at the concert. I think it was actually *seeing* them perform that moved me so.

I must say that watching the news every morning is improving my listening comprehension and my knowledge of Spanish affairs! Now they don't seem so sure about the economy and think it may grow more slowly than expected.

All these new golf complexes will soon be ready for the expected exodus from Northern Europe and there is increasing concern in some quarters that there won't be enough water to supply the houses, let alone water the courses. They occasionally give a minute's air time to a member of the 'Partido Verde' (Green Party), and those people are not at all happy about the state of affairs. One of them said that the government are irresponsible lunatics, but extremists do say extreme things. In any case, it is all the more reason to give up golf, which I have, in fact, given up already, but still dream about from time to time. I cannot control my subconscious.

Paco enjoyed singing 'King of the Road', and so did I; a rousing song! I feel that I can relate to Country and Western music more than to Flamenco music, even though I have no cowboy ancestry. We later talked about the economy, Paco saying that the central and regional governments were 'lunáticos irresponsables'. He said that there was little enough water for agriculture and that all this building was 'locura' (craziness). He said that Spain had always been a country of 'locos' (crazy people) and added that nothing good ever lasted. He suggested that I read some Spanish history, so I will. I don't know why I didn't think of it before.

Sábado, 26 de Enero

My day of Spanish history studies on the computer has been an illuminating one, and I am forced to agree with Paco's verdict. What a comedy of errors! I read about the building of an empire, the plundering of an empire, the loss of an empire, monarchies, republics, anarchy, dictatorships, wars, coups, more republics, dictatorships and monarchies, until it didn't seem to matter which century I was reading about. By the 1940s, Spain seemed to be back where it was in the fifteenth century and, after all the success of the last thirty or forty years, including democracy, they must surely be due for another catastrophe. I will watch the news with a new scepticism from now on. I suppose that now that Spain is in Europe, it will receive guidance from more sensible countries such as Britain.

Pamela has been at Laura's all afternoon. I am glad she is not neglecting her Spanish friendships.

Domingo, 27 de Enero

Cold and sunny. Pamela has once again got it into her head that I don't have enough to do to occupy my time and has suggested that we have a few days away. While heartily disagreeing with the first part of her statement (Spanish language studies? History studies? Shelf making? Weeding? Tending the wood-burning stove? Isn't that enough to occupy a man?), I agreed that a little 'road trip' was a splendid idea, and at once made for the computer to plan it. This has kept me busy for the rest of the day.

I have proposed that we make our first trip a cross-country ramble; by car, of course, to explore the area inland from Puebla de Don Arsenio. We will head westwards a little, before turning northwards and exploring some of the remoter settlements of inland Valencia. Then we will turn westwards again and visit the famous town of Cuenca with its 'hanging houses', before heading south and finally eastwards and home.

Cuenca is the only real tourist destination on our trip and is really a concession to Pamela, who would have preferred to visit Madrid or Barcelona. I have promised that on our second trip we will 'do' one of those cities, but that first I want to see some of the 'real' Spain. Pamela pointed out that we were living in the 'real' Spain, and I replied that I wished to compare and contrast. She said, "have it your own way," which I took to be an endorsement of my plan, albeit not an enthusiastic one. I will make the trip so interesting that she will thank me for taking her on it. We must, she says, wait for a good weather forecast, and she does not want to miss her Tuesday morning Line Dancing.

Martes, 29 de Enero

Raining today and more rain forecast. Yesterday I planned our trip down to the last detail, and now we must just wait for four days of good weather which don't include a Tuesday, the Sacred Day of Line Dancing. Indeed, Pamela returned from that activity today inordinately enthusiastic about it. The dancing was fun, she said, and she was meeting some very nice people. Dorothy, a nice lady from Lancashire, told her about an excellent car boot sale that takes place every Saturday in a village down towards the coast. There was also an expression of interest about my golf clubs from a lady from Leicester, who said that her husband would probably call me soon. Good!

As our trip cannot take place this week, I suggested that we take a look at the car boot sale on Saturday. Pamela agreed, but warned me that it was mainly a foreign affair, and I replied that I had suspected so all along, but that I must have books and would grin and bear the 'guiris'. I was delighted to find that Pamela did not know this word, so I tortured her, metaphorically speaking, with clues as to its meaning. I said, "You are one and are happy to be one, whereas I don't wish to be one." She guessed at 'woman', which I thought funny, and 'rational person', which she thought funny, before I told her the meaning, which she has now stored away with the rest of her immense vocabulary. It was nice to briefly know one word which she did not.

Half an hour looking for useful words that Pamela may not know, followed by half an hour of 'A Boy Named Sue'. This song is one long narrative and may have to be imparted in instalments.

Jueves, 31 de Enero

Cold, rainy and miserable. Our first winter is certainly dragging on and is of a severity that I did not expect. Pamela says that next winter will be much more bearable, as we will have central heating. She said this in such a matter of fact, almost 'fait accompli', manner that she rendered me speechless. No discussion, no weighing up of pros and cons; just the stating of a fact. Remarkable.

The insurance company telephoned and I passed them over to Pamela. They have given our car up for lost and wish to compensate us with the current value of the car. They stated a figure which was approximately three-quarters of what we paid for it in October; only four months ago! I rang back and demanded to speak to someone in English. After holding the line for several minutes, I was put through to a woman who spoke perfect English with a perfectly Spanish accent. I remonstrated that the car was as good as new and she said that that was as may be, but if one sold a car of that age, that is the price one would get. She then gave me a polite and lengthy explanation of the company policy, which could be summarised as 'take it or leave it'. They also want our little Japanese car back very soon.

These two events took place yesterday morning and I have been in a state of numbness ever since. The financial implications are disastrous and have put paid to my pre-pensions budgeting forecast. I have paid into two private pensions, as well as my paltry state pension, and I fear that a decade of penury awaits us.

A short while ago Pamela brought me a cup of tea and asked how long I was going to go on sulking. I told her that fifty-four year old men did not sulk and that I was merely readjusting my mind-set to cope with the poverty that awaited us. She told me not to be silly and that, thanks to her (late) mother, we could live comfortably until retirement age and beyond. This reference to her mother - a proud lady, who never took me entirely seriously - stung a little, but was not intended as an insult to my capacity as a provider.

I rallied a little before today's class and managed to impart half of 'A Boy Named Sue' in Paco's half hour. He was then too excited about the outcome of the narrative to concentrate on my Spanish, so we finished the song and he sobbed over his almond liqueur as he relived the happy ending. He is aware that next week the whole hour will be in Spanish.

Viernes, 1 de FEBRERO 2008

We have now been in Spain for a quarter of a year! What have I achieved? Well, my Spanish has improved notably and I am now able to understand normal, unhurried speech. I am also able to speak in a normal, slightly simplistic, unhurried way. I have now almost finished my Intermediate Spanish Grammar book and will run through it again before I progress onto the Advanced Spanish Grammar book which awaits me! I hope that while I am revising the first book, my spoken Spanish will do a little catching up. I chat in the bars, I chat in the shops, and I chat in a more structured way with Paco, but I would like to be able to have lengthier conversations without always having to perform Country and Western songs first. I *must* expand my Spanish social circle.

In other areas of my life, my horticulture has not been as active as I would have liked. I will reopen the book and see what I can plant this month, now that 'the brief winter' (estate agency literature) must be almost over. I am proud of my very straight shelves and Pamela's curtain rails and will find more DIY tasks to do soon.

Pamela also seems to be getting along fine. Her Spanish seems excellent and it must be true that knowing French makes it easier to learn. I did German at school, before putting my linguistic light under a bushel for almost forty years. I am a little concerned about her fraternising with the Line Dancing set and will myself continue to steer clear of English-speaking society, except for Andy.

And, of course, we have our first trip to look forward to, further trips, a visit from Gerald; and spring will soon be here!

Sábado, 2 de Febrero

Angeles called round this morning as we were getting ready to go to the car boot sale. Pamela has avoided her company lately, as she considers her a 'nattering, interfering, old crone'. She had brought some herbs in a plastic bag and explained to Pamela, while ignoring me, that they could be boiled to make tasty infusions. It was impressive to see how Pamela thanked her effusively, asked her how they both were, and skilfully steered her back out of the door, all in the space of two minutes. 'Deflective social skills' could be the term for it. I have also given up somewhat on Nora, as miming is still his main medium of communication with me. At least our other neighbours are more interesting, although they have yet to call on us. Pamela says the herbs are mint, rosemary and thyme. I too recognised the mint, by the smell.

The car boot sale took place on some spare ground on the outskirts of the neat little village. It looked like a shanty town added to the village and was nothing like the car boot sales I had attended in England, where small trestle tables and even actual car boots were the stalls. Here the stalls were proper stalls and just a few trestle tables, while the stall keepers and customers were of many nations, including Spain. There was junk of every variety and a lot of handsome articles too. Books were my target and, when Pamela bumped into a fellow line-dancer, I excused myself and commenced my hunt. I was tempted by a collection of The Famous Five novels, before reminding myself that I am no longer a young teenager. I picked up a 'Nicholas Nickleby' and a 'Great Expectations' and rued the fact that the Liverpudlian vendor said he had just sold a whole set of Dickens. That must be at least two feet of shelf space! I bought a thick atlas from a purple German and was paying for a guide to the Canary Islands from a very pale Spaniard when I spotted in the gloom of his van a set of encyclopedias! At my request, he pulled out a dusty volume and said that I could have that and the other seventy-one tomes of the 'Enciclopedia Espasa-Calpe' for €150. He allowed me into his van to inspect them, and came to see how I was getting on ten minutes later. Apart from a coffee or tea stain on the index page of volume thirty-four, I could see little wrong with them. He shook his head sadly at my offer of one hundred, but when I pointed out how much extra diesel his van would be using to lug them from one market to another, he lowered his price to €125. Done!

I made nine increasingly exhausting trips to the car and then started to look for Pamela to tell her the good news. I found her in a makeshift eatery with old Ernie of Line Dancing fame and several of his disciples. I had no option but to take coffee with them and must say that they were, on the whole, an agreeable group of ladies. Ernie was very chirpy and seemed to very much enjoy having his 'ménage' around him. He didn't appear to have designs on any of them, but you can never tell; he did walk a pudding-faced lady through some dance steps very attentively. I announced my recent acquisition and they all expressed polite interest, except for a Welsh woman who said, "What on earth do you want all them for?" A dyed in the wool expat, if ever I saw one.

Pamela had spotted a desk and chair that she thought would do very nicely for my study, so I hurried her away from the chattering dancers to show it to me. The young Moroccan (I presume) tending the stall must have seen my eagerness, for it was a beautiful desk, and asked €250 for it, throwing the chair in free. My previous haggling and carrying had tired me and I failed to knock him down more than €20. It wouldn't have fit in the silly little Japanese car anyway.

On returning home, I headed straight for the computer to search for asking prices for Espasa-Calpe encyclopedias. I saw prices of €500, €1000 and even €5000 for complete sets! Mine were a bargain indeed, I thought, and it was with great disappointment that I later discovered that volume sixty-two was missing. I feel too low to write more about this just now and consider the stall-holder to have been a very poor ambassador to Spain at the 'car boot sale'.

Lunes, 4 de Febrero

Two cloudy days, and it is only now that I am coming out from under my cloud of disappointment regarding volume sixty-two, for which I have searched on the internet with no success. I could return to the car boot sale to challenge the man, but I doubt he will dare to return there after such a heinous swindle. Pamela says that he probably didn't even know that volume sixty-two was missing, but I cannot believe that. I will be missing every Spanish word between 'Tiro' and 'Toun' until I track down a volume, but console myself with the fact that I have plenty to be going on with in the meantime. The encyclopedia occupies two whole shelves and gives a very scholarly aspect to my study.

Today I have turned my attention to the subject of our new car. I fear it will have to be second-hand, as my heart is set on an estate car, which are considerably more expensive than our purloined Seat Ibiza. Had I already had an estate car, that exquisite desk would now be in my study. Furthermore, all serious DIY and horticulture buffs own estate cars, usually topped off with sturdy roof-racks. The Spanish second-hand car market is not as well-organised as that of England, and I will first consult my friends, Andy and Paco, for advice. Writing that sentence reminds me that, as yet, I only have two friends in Spain, and one is Scottish. Practically all my friends in England were golfers and this easy source of companionship is to be denied me here. Food for thought, but no matter.

This afternoon I read about 'abadías' (abbeys) in the encyclopedia, and tomorrow I will tackle 'abanicos' (fans – those for fanning yourself with). Fascinating stuff, and extremely in depth.

Miércoles, 6 de Febrero

With Pamela's Line Dancing out of the way for another week, and in view of the relatively mild weather forecast, I proposed yesterday that we set off on our 'road trip' today. She said that she was *so* looking forward to getting our new car, whichever it may be, that she would prefer to wait until we had it, rather than go in 'that nasty little Japanese thing'; her words, but true. Pamela has never attached any importance to cars, even being indifferent to my joy on changing our old Volvo for a nearly new Saab, and I suspect that this is a ruse to delay the trip until the spring. This crafty ploy spurred me to call on Andy after lunch to ask his advice on motoring matters.

He was in his large greenhouse, plying his 'azada' with a vengeance, when I arrived, but downed tools immediately and hurried out to greet me. I didn't recognise the crop he was digging around, although it looked familiar, but I didn't want to show my ignorance by asking him what it was. He made me a coffee and told me that he knew a man who was 'the man' for second-hand cars in Villeda, and said he would introduce me to him tomorrow. I asked him if the man was trustworthy and Andy said that, in general terms, he was not, but that if he, Andy, asked him to pick out a good car for a good friend, he would do so. "Clueless customers get the knackers," he said.

I spent one hour reading about 'abanicos' and 'abdicación' earlier. Fans were fun, but I found the subject of abdication very hard going. Pamela says that I will have to live to a hundred to read the whole encyclopedia, to which I replied, "Only ninety-nine if I don't find volume sixty-two," which I thought funny and sad at the same time.

Viernes, 8 de Febrero

Yesterday morning, Andy and I drove into town to see the second-hand car salesman. He, Arturo by name, was a very big man with a very small forecourt. He was exhibiting a stock of around a dozen cars, on his forecourt and on the street outside, and when Andy said that I was 'un amigo de verdad' ('a true friend' – I liked that) the options narrowed to just three. One of these was a large, dark brown Peugeot estate with an impressive roof-rack, which I fell in love with immediately. Arturo was pleased with my choice and said it was 'un diesel robusto', while Andy pointed out that it was twenty years old. Arturo said that it had a mere 165,000 kilometres on the clock - nothing for a diesel - and that he had not had time to tamper with it, which I thought very honest of him to tell me. Andy said that it looked like an oversized coffin and that Pamela would not be at all pleased. I said that I would just like to take a little test drive and that I would weigh up the pros and cons very carefully before making a decision.

When I arrived home in the Peugeot, Pamela laughed and said that it looked like a huge coffin. She assumed that I had borrowed it, as the tiny Japanese car was being recalled by the insurance company, and became very quiet when I told her that I had bought it. Andy said that he had done what he could but that, "the twerp wouldn't be shifted."

Pamela maintained a stolid silence at lunch, while I extolled the virtues of the car: space, comfort, the economy of the 2.5 litre diesel engine (compared to a 2.5 litre petrol engine), the likelihood that in an accident any normal car would come off much worse, and it's very low price. Over coffee she cleared her throat and finally spoke, saying that she was very glad that the 'monstrosity' had been cheap, because she intended to purchase a small car for herself, and that she wouldn't be seen *dead* in that 'gypsy wagon'. I begged her not to be racialist as our virtuoso neighbours were gypsies and she said, almost shouted in fact, "Racist, you fool, not racialist!" At the time of writing, one day later, her only words since then have been 'yes', 'no' and 'never'. I shall visit the trinket shop tomorrow, or even the jeweller's.

Not in the best of spirits, I found the subject of abdomens uninspiring reading and have decided that from now on I will 'dip into' the encyclopedia as and when I wish. This, after all, is their conventional use.

A pleasant drive into town this morning in my splendid car! On starting up, it is reminiscent of Paco's tractor, but soon quietens down to a smooth purr when out on the road with the windows closed. The power steering is excellent, and probably very necessary, and with the back seats down it could easily carry a cow, lying down. I bought a bead necklace for Pamela, as her muted civility at breakfast dispelled my fears that it would have to be something of silver or gold. She accepted it with a smile and said it was a, "blatant and unimaginative peace offering," but that she was sorry that she had overreacted to my purchase of the car. It was, she said, simply the shock of seeing the most unimaginably ugly thing on four wheels and the realisation that it belonged to us and not to a family heading west in a Steinbeck novel. I shall look up Steinbeck in the encyclopedia to see what she might be referring to.

Paco called round this afternoon to apologise for missing this week's class (because there was to be no Country and Western song?) and to see the car which he said was 'the talk of the village'. People, he said, could not understand why the 'wealthy foreigners' would buy such an old, enormous and unfashionable car, although he himself liked it very much, especially the sound of the engine. I pointed out that, although we were undoubtedly foreigners, we were not wealthy and that I would be grateful if he would dispel any rumours of riches that may be circulating around the village. We wanted to be just another village family, I told him, scraping a living off the land. He said he would try, and that us having that old 'tanque' of a car would help. I hope Pamela does not insist on buying herself a new one.

Martes, 12 de Febrero

My first journal entry for three days! This is all right, I tell myself, as it is not a diary and February is a maudlin month. That is alliteration, I believe, and when I review the journal prior to publication, I will insert more of it. In fact, I will start seriously striving to select some suitable samples of sublime and serendipitous sentences now - ha! I like that and have now looked up serendipitous, and it makes sense.

Yesterday it occurred to me that Pamela would need to transport herself to her Line Dancing today and that it would be a good opportunity to persuade her to take her first ride in the car, which she insists on referring to as 'el ataúd' (the coffin). She was adamant on catching the bus and I had to practically beg her to let me take her in the car. She insisted that she was perfectly capable of driving any car herself, but I said that for a lady of slightly under average height it would take some getting used to. She called me a 'sexualist', but agreed to let me occupy the passenger seat for her first and possibly last drive, as she has already asked Ana to ask Andy to ask 'that charlatan Arturo' to find her a reliable small car, preferably made in the present century.

She looked very small behind the wheel - she is almost a foot shorter than me - but after adjusting the seat and the mirrors, she started the engine confidently enough. She said that it sounded, and felt, like a tractor and that I should give it to Paco for his birthday. She drove it competently into town and eventually found a parking space large enough to contain it. I asked her what she thought of it and she said that it felt like driving a barge, although I know for a fact that she has never driven one, unless it was during her mysterious year in Paris.

I browsed in the Ferretería for a while and then called in at the quaint little bookshop to ask if they would be able to obtain volume sixty-two of the 1929 edition of the Espasa-Calpe encyclopedia for me. The polite lady blinked several times before answering that she didn't have one in the shop, but that she would ask all her contacts in the book trade to try to locate one for me. I bought (in Spanish, of course) a copy of 'The Grapes of Wrath', which is by that Steinbeck fellow, to show my appreciation of her good intentions. Perhaps this is what she intended with her good intentions, I later reflected.

Pamela said that Marjorie, the lady from Leicester, was surprised that her husband had not called me, as he was very much interested in speaking to me about golf. "Golf, or golf clubs?" I asked, suspicious of his designs. "Golf clubs, golf, what's the difference?" she replied. I told her that it was the difference between abstinence and renewed addiction! She gave me one of her roguish smiles and told me to wait and see. I will stand firm and will not be led down the garden path, or fairway, to expat golfing.

On the beautifully smooth drive home, myself once again at the wheel, I suggested that we set off on our road trip tomorrow, but Pamela said that a new cold snap was forecast. She did acquiesce to going in the Peugeot, however, when the weather got a little warmer, which is a step in the right direction. She begins to recognise the merits of our sturdy vehicle.

Miércoles, 13 de Febrero

It was chilly getting out of bed this morning and, what should I see on opening the curtains, but SNOW! I shook the slumbering Pamela and beckoned her to the window. She agreed that it was snow, told me to get the stove stoked up right away, and disappeared back under the duvet. I was thrilled that it had actually snowed in Spain, albeit only half an inch, and took photographs of the plot to prove it. Later, over coffee in the rustic bar, a very old man told me that today's snow was nothing; that back in the fifties, snowdrifts regularly blocked the front door of his hovel. Exaggeration? Global warming? Senility? I don't know.

The few children in the village certainly enjoyed it while it lasted and pelted me with snowballs on my way to the bakery, shouting, "guiri, guiri, guiri!" as they did so. It is always good to see youthful high spirits, but I felt that they showed a worrying lack of deference to their elders, in this case me, and one snowball hit me square on the nose. I shall not speak to their parents this time, but I know who two of them belong to and will be on the alert for further signs of disrespect.

Pamela was not as thrilled about the snow as I, and reminded me to phone the wood-man, which I am now able to do myself. I asked her if she seriously believed that we needed central heating and she put her extremely cold hand inside my shirt by way of reply, before going to Laura's from where she has yet to return.

I am finding the Steinbeck novel hard going, but can now see how Pamela conjured up her curious 'heading west' image. They would, I feel sure, have been far more comfortable in my Peugeot.

Viernes, 15 de Febrero

What will hopefully be the last really cold spell of weather has ended today and it is warm in the sun. I feel that Paco did not enjoy our exclusively Spanish class yesterday; not due to not wishing to converse with me, but to his pining for the twang of a country guitar. We conversed about horticulture, and he seems to be overly fond of the use of chemicals. When I asked him about the different crops that I could plant, he reeled off a list of the hormones that I must use on them and the pesticides that I must douse them with. I found his desire to dominate the plant kingdom a little unsettling, and it does not sound very healthy at all. I doubted that they would be necessary for my little plot and resolved to ask Andy for advice on what to plant next.

I was polishing my car this morning when, to my surprise, I saw that very man coming out of Rocío and Pedro's house. He said that he had taken them a few herbs and, on noting my puzzled expression, said, "Marijuana. You saw the plants in my greenhouse, didn't you?" On seeing me struck dumb, he proceeded to reassure me that I shouldn't believe everything I had read in the Tory papers and that it was a pleasant, harmless drug when consumed in moderation. He added that my neighbour Pedro derived much inspiration for his guitar compositions from the 'benign weed'. I said that, firstly, I had been an Independent reader and, secondly, that if it was illegal there must be a good reason for it. He laughed and asked me if it was all right to drink two bottles of whisky every day, as that was a perfectly legal thing to do. I saw the sense in this - the statement, not the whisky drinking - but was still shocked when he told me that he and Ana occasionally enjoyed a relaxing 'spliff' of an evening. Ana too! That a rascally Scotsman should transgress the law of the land was one thing, but for the angelic Ana to sully herself with illicit substances was quite another. I asked him if he did not fear a 'raid' from the police and he laughed and said, "Yes, the local police often pop round to take samples." He tried to convince me that there was a greater tolerance to 'grass' smoking in Spain, but the internet states that it is equally illegal here, and the thought of the lovely Ana behind bars chills my heart.

I postponed asking him for advice on what to plant on my plot and he went on his way. Pamela took this revelation very calmly and suggested that I might like to try it sometime, adding that I would have to smoke an awful lot to get as 'high' as I did at the barbecue. That blessed barbecue will haunt me forever.

Domingo, 17 de Febrero

A mild weekend and a quiet one. On resuming my horticultural studies yesterday, I was disappointed to find that I should already have started planting tomatoes, peppers, lettuces, celery, aubergines and cucumber; all in planting trays and in a warm environment. I can achieve the warm environment, next to the stove, but light would be lacking. My first impulse was to hurtle off somewhere to buy a greenhouse, but Pamela urged calm and, more effectively, economy. She suggested I ring Andy to ask his advice, but I have not assimilated his transgressions sufficiently to speak to him yet.

Half an hour reading about Steinbeck's dysfunctional family and half an hour of words to 'Stand By Your Man'.

Lunes, 18 de Febrero

Andy called round this morning as I was polishing the car and handed me a brochure. A little bird - Pamela, of course - had told him that my fingers were becoming green once more, and he explained that the 'viverista' (nursery) on the road to Alicante would meet my spring planting requirements, but that I must wait a month before purchasing and replanting on my plot. He would supply me with some young tomato plants, he said, and a patch of 'María' would look well down near the track. Before I could ask him what 'Maria' was, he burst out laughing and said, "Not for a square like yourself, I fear." "Better to be square than enclosed in a square cell!" I retorted, which I thought rather sharp.

We had a cup of coffee and leafed through the 'viverista' brochure, which included some beautiful greenhouses. Andy said to first see how I took to it this year, before splashing out on one, as working the land wasn't everybody's cup of tea. I told him that it was most certainly going to be my cup of tea, as that was the main reason we were here. "Speak for yourself," said Pamela from the kitchen.

I looked up 'marijuana' in the encyclopedia, but the brief reference to it was purely scientific. I assume that this hateful hallucinogen (nice alliteration) was not consumed until more recent and depraved times.

Martes, 19 de Febrero

At last we are to set off on our first road trip - tomorrow! Now I am far too busy packing and doing last minute research to write much. I shall take a notebook with me and synthesise my notes into a noteworthy journal entry when we return. Pamela's words of 'let's get it over with' have made me even more determined that it will be an enjoyable and informative trip.

Domingo, 24 de Febrero

Where to begin? The trip was, all things considered, a qualified success. Pamela says we are going to Madrid next - straight to Madrid. She only put it that way because I don't believe that she fully grasped the purpose of our exploratory journey, which was not at all the 'aimless meandering' she called it one lengthy afternoon. The future reader will decide, after reading the following 'travel notes':

Day One (Miércoles):
La Puebla de Don Arsenio to El Rincón de Ademuz (Valencia)

We left the village at ten this morning and, after filling the disturbingly large fuel tank at the petrol station in town, we 'hit the road'. We took the Madrid motorway - more a dual carriageway, really - as far as Almansa, where we made our first scheduled stop. The fourteenth century castle was the main reason for our visit and it was very different to most of the British castles I have seen. I was much impressed by its impeccable condition until I came across a builder trowelling cement into a turret. This is cheating, as I don't believe cement was one of the original building materials. Pamela thought it very trim and tidy, but I felt that it lacked the 'mystique' of proper ruined castles. No such spruceness was in evidence at the foot of the castle, where many of the houses *were* in a state of ruin, and a pair of demented eyes which viewed us from one of them sent Pamela scurrying for the car. After a pleasant, economical, 'menú del día' lunch of chops, chips and salad in a roadside restaurant in the town, marred only by the loud television, we took the main road to Requena.

We made good progress to Ayora, with its fittingly ruined castle, but after that the main road became a very narrow and twisty one, on which tractors and lorries slowed our progress considerably. The earth became redder, the land poorer, and the villages, which looked so picturesque from a distance, were rather shabby at closer quarters. The village of Cofrentes was much nicer though, and, as Pamela was complaining of a sore bottom, we stopped for a coffee. I complemented a man in the bar on the neatness of his village and asked him how the people made a living there. He asked me if I had seen the big chimneys in the valley, and I said that I had. "Our lovely nuclear power station," he said. "That's how we make a living. That and the 'guilt money' they give to the council." He 'humphed', finished his brandy, and left the bar. Spain is full of surprises.

The land flattened and the road straightened as we approached Requena, and I told the grumbling and fidgeting Pamela that on these good roads we should reach our destination in a little over half an hour. After speeding along at 50mph for a while, the road became very twisty again and, when I asked Pamela how she was, she said, "I feel sick and this stupid old car has numbed my arse." Pamela swearing, which she rarely does, is a warning sign which I heeded by staying silent until we reached Ademuz shortly after nightfall.

We checked into the two star 'Hotel Casa Paco' and were shown to our room by a spotty, sullen youth. Pamela told me to run the bath, order her a beer, and leave her alone for a while, which I did. We later had a pleasant dinner of steak, chips and salad in the modern dining room, marred only by the loud television. I assured Pamela that tomorrow we had a relatively short drive to the beautiful village of Tragacete. She said that she wished to spend no more than one hour in 'that rumbling crate' and I promised that an hour - an hour and a quarter at the most - was all it would take us.

Day Two (Jueves):
El Rincón de Ademuz to Tragacete

A cold but sunny start to the day. Ademuz is a pleasant village and the arrival of a coach-load of pensioners pleased me, as it proved that it was indeed a tourist destination and not the 'freezing, godforsaken place' that Pamela had called it the night before. Unhappily for Pamela, and consequently for me, the road to Tragacete was even more twisty and torturous than yesterday's. The fifty-five miles to Tragacete, due to the nature of the road and the intransigence of tractor drivers, took us over three hours, and the fact that Pamela said she was 'thoroughly pissed off' proved beyond doubt that she was. She was unwilling or unable to appreciate the beauty of the scenery, or the village, and, when we pulled up outside the nondescript modern hotel where we were to spend the night, she said, "It is three o'clock. We are at an ugly hotel in a tiny village and after I have recovered from that horrible drive it will be dark. Wait here." Some minutes later she re-emerged from the hotel and, to my surprise, signalled me into the driver's seat. "It is an hour to Cuenca," she said, "and I would rather die of bum ache than stay here. Drive!"

She didn't die of 'bum ache' because she lay down in the back of the car, thus missing yet more lovely scenery, and I drove to Cuenca on a very narrow, winding road, without sharing with her my concern over the rapidly plummeting fuel gauge needle. We made it, just, and my calculations suggest that the car drinks diesel like a fish drinks water - if they do actually drink a lot of it, which I don't know - which is most annoying.

As we had reached Cuenca one day earlier than scheduled, we had no hotel reservation and Pamela once again took it upon herself to ask advice of total strangers rather than adapting my carefully planned itinerary. After speaking at length to a well-dressed lady, she got back in the car and directed me along the street and up a hill to what looked like a monastery. It is in fact a 'Parador Nacional', a state-sponsored hotel, which had been built as a convent in the sixteenth century. It is extremely grand and cannot be cheap, but Pamela has forbidden me from worrying about the price, so I will try not to. We have a fine view across the gorge of the old part of Cuenca and what I presume to be the famous 'hanging houses'. As far as I can see, they do not actually 'hang' at all, but merely have balconies over the gorge, which is not the same thing at all.

We had a fine dinner, including a very tasty dish called 'Zarajos', which the waiter later told us contained lamb's intestines. He said that he always told foreign guests this fact afterwards, so that they would not miss out on the exquisite dish through squeamishness. We drank a bottle of superb 'Ribera del Duero' red wine and Pamela seemed her old cheerful self once more. I suggested that we make a rapid tour of the old town tomorrow morning, before resuming our itinerary, but she said no, we would spend all day in Cuenca, as they were plenty of things to see. We would stay in this wonderful Parador for another night, and then we would drive home on the *straightest* roads the following day. I saw by the imperative nature of her words that this is, in fact, what we will be doing, so I did not protest.

Day Three (Viernes):
Just Cuenca

Today *has* been a pleasant day and any feelings of regret at forsaking my itinerary were tempered by remembering how much diesel that car consumes. Arturo likened the car to 'un mechero' (a lighter) in reference to its economy, but I think a huge blowtorch would be a better analogy. We visited the 'hanging houses', which don't hang at all, in which there is an abstract art museum; more Pamela's cup of tea than mine. Later we saw inside the impressive Gothic cathedral and had lunch in a restaurant in a pleasant square. I asked the waiter if they provided a 'menú del día', to which he laughed and said, "No need cheap menú. Cuenca tourist city." This was disappointing, but we were able to sit outside, thanks to the clever under-table heaters, and thus avoided the loud television marring our lunch again. We walked back to the Parador across the famous San Pablo Bridge, which is not old, being made of iron, but very vertiginous. I had to stop for a moment and grip the rail, as I was feeling a little dizzy, but Pamela said that being a passenger in 'that hideous contraption' was far worse. Rather than eating more intestines, I tried the strangely named dish, 'Atascaburras' - roughly translated as 'Clogger Up of Donkeys' - which was a delicious concoction of potatoes, cod, boiled egg and walnuts, and did not clog me up at all. Pamela promised that she would make it for me one day and said she had very much enjoyed our day in Cuenca. It has been a typically touristy day and I am not a typical tourist, but it has been pleasurable all the same.

Day Four (Sábado):
Cuenca to La Puebla de Don Arsenio

After paying our astronomical hotel bill and filling up with many gallons of diesel, we headed for home. Pamela, without consulting the map, said that she expected to keep seeing signs for La Roda until we reached La Roda, and that from there on we were not to leave the motorway until almost home. Her having consulted strangers regarding our route showed a distinct lack of belief in my promise that we would take the quickest and straightest route home, which, coupled with the stunning blow of the hotel bill, made *me* very quiet and pensive on this leg of our trip. Pamela chirped away about the delights of Cuenca, saying how much she was looking forward to us spending a few days in Madrid, visiting all the museums and other sights, and perhaps going to the theatre or the opera. I watched the fuel gauge needle descend as she spoke. I will take the car to the garage for diagnosis next week.

So, as I said, the trip was a qualified success. The 'road trip' turned into a more traditional, more static, type of excursion on reaching Cuenca, after which Pamela seemed to become much happier. I will bear this in mind when planning our future travels around Spain.

Martes, 26 de Febrero

After driving Pamela to Line Dancing, I drove round to see Arturo about the car's phenomenal fuel consumption. On telling him where we had been, he laughed and said that the route I had taken was not the most conducive to economical driving. I told him that it had guzzled equally thirstily on the motorway at eighty kilometres per hour, to which he shrugged and said that it was an old car with a big engine. I said that I thought he had said that it was a 'mechero', and he replied that it was, relatively speaking. I wanted to reply, 'Yes, compared to a blowtorch!' but did not know the word for blowtorch. (It is 'soplete', I now know.) The Peugeot's key characteristics have certainly changed in his eyes since it became my property. I shall take it to a proper garage for tests.

Pamela enjoyed her Line Dancing, as always, and said that the other ladies had been keen to hear about our trip, as none of them had been to Cuenca (because they are expats, I thought). She said that she had told them about the good and bad parts of the trip, and that Nerys (that Welsh woman) thought that I was 'bonkers' for wanting to traipse around all those little roads. Marjorie from Leicester said that her husband was sure to call me this week, as he was now sure that he could say what he wanted to say to me. This seemed very enigmatic, but Pamela was unable or unwilling to shed any light on the strange statement. He either wants to buy the golf clubs or he doesn't, and if he is planning to borrow them, he will be disappointed.

One hour reading about Cuenca in the encyclopedia and ten minutes regretting that I will not be able to read about Toledo until I track down volume sixty-two.

Jueves, 28 de Febrero

The weather has warmed up considerably and I am itching to do horticultural things. I rashly pulled up an onion and immediately wished I hadn't, as it was very underdeveloped, so I left the potatoes well alone. Patience and faith in Mother Nature, Ernest! Andy says that he will bring his rotavator round when it is time to pay a visit to the viverista, so I will wait for his cue.

Paco and I performed a wonderful rendition of 'Stand By Your Man' and I do believe that we are beginning to develop simple harmonies. We chuckled over the translation of the song and Paco said it was good that some women still knew their place. Pamela popped her head round the study door and asked us if we were feeling a little queer. It was not easy to explain this 'double entendre' to Paco, but Pamela's advanced Spanish was up to the task. Paco answered that, while he was certainly not gay, he had become so engrossed in the song that he had momentarily forgotten if he was a man or a woman. Pamela also pointed out the subtle irony of the song, which had completely escaped us.

Viernes, 29 de Febrero (because 2008 is an 'año bisiesto')

'When February's extra day is as warm as today, life is child's play.'

That is a little rhyme that I thought up this morning while I was standing in the bakery 'queue'! Perhaps I will begin to write poetry when I am a little older and less busy. A third of a year has passed since we took up residence in our as yet nameless house. Nameless, but not for long, as my latest name submission to Pamela has received a 'hmm' of approval. 'Casa Integración' (Integration House) is the name, and I feel that it sums up our intentions - and, I must say, partial achievement - wonderfully. Pamela jokingly handed me a marker pen, but I must now look seriously into *how* the name is to appear. Ceramic tiles? Wood? Wrought iron? This only adds to my ever growing list of important tasks, but it will be well worth the effort when I see it placed over, or next to, the front door!

Sábado, 1 de MARZO 2008

A mild start to this much awaited month! Today I had a most unexpected telephone call from Line Dancing Marjorie's husband. The call itself was expected, and feared, but what I did not imagine in a million years was that Marjorie's husband would be called Alfredo and that he is, in fact, Spanish! He addressed me in very rudimentary English and had obviously prepared his speech beforehand, imagining, wrongly, that I would not understand Spanish. He wants us to meet and to talk about playing golf together. I didn't even know that Spanish people played golf, apart from famous ones like Seve Ballesteros and a handful of others, but it seems they do, or at least Alfredo does, and he thinks we would enjoy playing and chatting together.

Pamela then told me that Marjorie had met Alfredo ten years ago in Madrid, where she was working as a language teacher and translator. At that time she already spoke excellent Spanish and they have spoken Spanish to each other ever since. On hearing from Marjorie that an English friend's husband was a golfer, Alfredo was immediately keen to meet him. Pamela then added that she assumed that I would decline the offer, as I was so set on giving up the sport, but I said that Alfredo being Spanish made it a whole new ball game. "It's still golf," she said, but I replied that native golf and expat golf were two very different things. I would be improving my Spanish as I played and, as Alfredo was probably a novice, I would not take the game too seriously and become obsessed by it, again. She wished to know how I knew that Alfredo would be a novice and I said that it stood to reason; we have been playing the game for well over a hundred years, while golf courses have only recently begun to mushroom in Spain.

One hour reading about golf in the encyclopedia - a short entry, as expected, as in 1929 Spaniards could not even watch it on television - and half an hour polishing my clubs, irons and custom-made putter.

Lunes, 3 de Marzo

The mild weather continues. My much anticipated meeting with Alfredo took place this afternoon and, when we get one point clear, I am sure we shall get on splendidly. I will explain, or illustrate, the issue.

Alfredo arrived at the house at 5pm and, when I opened the door, he shook my hand vigorously and said, "Hello, you are Ernest, I am Alfredo. I am very pleased to meet you. I look forward to play golf and speak with you." He had obviously rehearsed this flawed little speech for me, and I replied in correct Spanish that I was also pleased to meet him and was looking forward to playing golf and speaking to him. He said, "Yes, yes," and I said, "Sí, sí," and we were silent for a while. I asked him, in Spanish, what he would like to drink, and he said, in English, that he would like a coffee. As I handed him the coffee I said, "Aquí tienes," and he replied, "Thank you very much." I heard Pamela suppress a laugh in the next room.

We sipped our coffee in a smiling silence, as if weighing each other up, before agreeing, in our respective languages of choice, to meet here on Saturday morning before driving to *his* golf club to play our first game. I said, "Adiós," and he said, "Goodbye," and when I closed the door, Pamela came into the room in tears - tears of laughter, of course.

I was a little indignant that he had insisted on addressing me in English when we do, in fact, live in a Spanish speaking country - Spain. She said that as he and Marjorie had always found it so natural to speak in Spanish, he had neglected to learn English properly for many years. On hearing about a golfing Englishman, he had resolved to seize the opportunity to practise while he played. On Saturday I will stand firm and not a single English word will pass my lips.

Two hours of Spanish golfing vocabulary.

Miercoles, 5 de Marzo

After driving Pamela to Line Dancing yesterday, I took the car to the garage which Paco had recommended as having the best car and tractor repairmen in the area. I had requested one hour of their time over the phone and the moustachioed mechanic got straight to work. He opened the bonnet and asked me to accelerate the car vigorously while he observed the engine and the exhaust fumes. He took the wheel and drove us around the block, making several sharp accelerations and nodding pensively. Finally, he connected a tube to the exhaust pipe and took some readings, before telling me that the car was fine and asking me for €30. I insisted that the car was not fine and told him how much diesel it had consumed on our trip. He said that I could expect no better from such a big old car and held out his hand. I shook it, but he held it out again for his money. All this happened very quickly and I shall tell Paco that the Mexican mechanic charged me at a rate of €180 per hour.

After fuming quietly in the car for a while, I collected Pamela from Line Dancing and told her how the mechanic had deceived me. She suggested that I trade the car in and buy a sensible one instead, which I may have to do, as every press of the accelerator pedal makes me cringe. Pamela says that Marjorie says that Alfredo is very much looking forward to our game of golf on Saturday and expects it to be a 'social' game, as I am an older man and have not played for a while. I, on the other hand, expect it to be competitive, especially regarding the language we speak, although I would also like to win the game.

After much investigation on the internet today, I have decided that our house name will be a wooden one. It will look better than painted tiles, and wrought iron would be far too expensive due to the large number of letters. Spanish internet lags far behind the English-speaking one, and I may have to order the sign from Britain, which I would rather not do, preferring to patronise local craftsmen. I will ask Andy for advice, as Paco's recommendations are not to be trusted.

One hour of golf vocabulary yesterday, and one hour perusing Spanish golfing internet sites today. It appears that a number of Spanish people have, in fact, taken up the game.

Jueves, 6 de Marzo

Light rain today - just what the plot needs. All the talk on the TV news is about Sunday's general election. I gather that the two main parties are similar to our Conservative and Labour parties and that, as the economy is performing so well, the 'socialists' (PSOE party) will probably get in again. I am taking little interest in these elections as I am not allowed to vote. This is not fair, as in Britain a Spaniard could practically get off the plane and walk straight to the polling station, after perhaps dropping in at the dole office first. Perhaps they will have the decency to let me vote next time.

In today's class, after translating and performing 'Walking After Midnight', we talked about golf. I tried out some of my golfing terms on Paco, but I think they were double-Dutch to him. He disapproves of the game, as the courses use a phenomenal amount of water which is needed for agriculture, and I think he is disappointed that I am going to play on Saturday.

I tried to say that it was just a one-off, for old times' sake, but I really hope that it won't be. That depends on the outcome of Saturday's battle for linguistic supremacy. In any case, I will not mention golf to Paco again, as it makes him as sad as some of the songs we study. He asked me if I had taken the car to the garage, and I said that I had, and that I felt that they had overcharged me somewhat. He said that the 'Mexican' mechanic, who is in fact from Seville, was the best in the business and that he would ask him about my car when he next took his tractor in for servicing.

Sábado, 8 de Marzo

I will not say that my first game of golf in Spain was a qualified success, as I believe I have used that term in the journal before and wish to avoid boring the future reader with boring repetition. Nevertheless, it was a qualified success.

After greeting each other bilingually, we drove to the golf

course in Alfredo's lovely BMW car. He said, "New car. Diesel. Very economic." and I said, "Sí, buen coche," and thought about my wretched machine. The course lay towards the coast; an artificial oasis in a scrubby area of land, and I was glad that Paco was not there to see the high powered water sprinklers. There were a mix of nationalities bustling around outside the modern club house and Paco greeted some Spanish players in Spanish; the first time I had heard him speak it. When he introduced me to a man called Juan in English and Juan said, "Pleased to meet you, Ernest," my infuriation was hard to contain and undoubtedly affected my first tee shot, which I sliced into the rough. Alfredo saying, "Bad luck. You long time not play," before hitting a magnificent drive, did little to settle my nerves. He holed in five, to my nine, and said, "Matchplay better for you today, yes?"

After seven holes I was seven holes down and was also coming a poor second in the language match, Alfredo having an endless supply of stock platitudes. It was on the eighth that I decided on a change of tactics. When he said, "Three iron better this short hole for you," I told him that I disagreed and that a five wood was my preferred choice for this kind of hole, and that I had had a soft spot for the 'five' ever since I took third place in my old club's knock-out tournament in '97, when old Jonesy clinched the win with a flukish birdie at the fifteenth - all this in English. He said, "Yes, yes. Five wood good," and I launched into the story of when Johnny Maxwell failed fourteen times to get out of a bunker on the eleventh and then holed from his fifteenth attempt. Alfredo said, "Yes, bunkers bad," and sent his tee shot into one.

From then on, I kept up a relentless stream of golfing comments, anecdotes and jokes, while Alfredo's golf went from bad to worse to absolutely shocking. By the fourteenth, I had run out of stories and improvised some of P.G.Wodehouse's 'Oldest Member' tales for him. Leaving the seventeenth green, I was one shot ahead and, as Alfredo grimly teed up for the last hole, I said, "Buena suerte," and lapsed into silence for the first time in an hour. He looked at me through leaden eyes and just said, "Gracias," whether for wishing him good luck or for finally shutting up, I cannot say. He drove straight as an arrow and won the hole by a shot. We were both satisfied with a draw, after quite possibly the most devilish game of golf I have ever played. I am not generally a devilish person, but golf, and language, can bring out the worst in me.

Over a beer in the clubhouse, Alfredo laughed at my diabolical destruction of his game and said, "Eres un cabrón," which means, 'You are a bastard', but in a nice way. We both realised that our linguistic requirements could only be met if we agreed to play the nine holes out in one language, and the nine holes back in the other. I asked him if he liked Country and Western music, but he does not.

Alfredo would not accept a penny, or cent, towards the day's expenses, but said that he would like to go in my car next time, as it brought back memories of the car his grandfather used to pick him up from school in when he was a child.

Domingo, 9 de Marzo

The PSOE have won the elections, so the one without the beard will be president. As a voiceless, vote-less citizen, I merely report this fact as a matter of general interest. Pamela has told me that I will be able to vote in municipal and

European elections, and that in the local ones I could even stand for office! I had never considered a career in politics, but who knows what the future will bring?

Ana and Andy came to lunch today and enjoyed the 'Atascaburras' that Pamela made for us. I told them the story of yesterday's game of golf, which Andy found especially funny, saying, "You really flummoxed the dago git." I looked at Ana when he said this and she just shrugged and said, "His little Scottish ways." She is very patient and must love him very much indeed to put up with such gross speech, although Pamela says that he does it on purpose because I am such a prude. I hope that Ana has more influence over their future child's development than he does.

Over coffee he took out a leather pouch and said, "Anyone for a spliff?" I did not jump at the bait, but instead said, "No, I usually have my heroin injection at five," which no-one found funny at all. Spontaneous humour may not be one of my strong points. Andy, after putting his pouch away, recommended that I order the wooden house name on the internet, making it very clear to them that there is an accent over the 'o' in 'Integración'. He said that if I asked a local 'chippy' to do it, he would spend a fortnight chiselling away and then charge me a fortune. I agreed, and was about to mention how his friend Arturo had misled me regarding the car's fuel consumption, but then remembered that he had tried to dissuade me from buying the thing in the first place. Better not to leave myself open to more of Andy's teasing, I thought.

Andy will bring the rotavator round one day soon and has promised to let me use it this time, as I am keen to do all the work on my plot with my own hands. I have already compiled my 'lista para la viverista'.

Martes, 11 de Marzo

Pamela went to Line Dancing on the bus today. She said she fancied a change, but also added that the car brought back uncomfortable memories. I may sell it soon, as it no longer gives me the pleasure that it once did. This afternoon I received a call, the first for a long time, from our interpreter. He reminded me of the small administrative issues that he had spoken to me about when we moved in, and said that he would like to meet me at the town hall on Thursday to discuss these slight anomalies with the relevant official.

I don't like his habit of always stressing the diminutive nature of these 'issues', and now feel a trifle uneasy. Since we have been here, thanks to my foresight before the move, all administrative matters have run very smoothly. We have our identity cards and our health cards, and our bills arrive and are paid punctually. While I sympathise with the 'horror stories' which some foreigners have experienced, I feel that my scrupulous management of our domestic affairs has effectively prevented us from suffering the same fate as these unfortunate, probably thoroughly disorganised, people. On Thursday we shall see.

One hour studying Spanish municipal legislation on the internet. I cannot make head nor tale of it.

Jueves, 13 de Marzo

I arrived at the town hall at 10 o'clock and greeted our interpreter, Miguel; a young, pale man who must not get out of doors much, in Spanish. He showed polite astonishment at my linguistic progress and asked after Pamela and the house, before switching to English. I did not mind this because that, after all, is what I am paying him for. The official, a young lady, was expecting us and led us into her small office.

She bade us be seated and began to explain the situation to Miguel. I understood half of what she was saying, nodding to prove it, but listened carefully to Miguel's interpretation, as I suspected that it was somewhere in the half that I didn't understand where the crux of the matter lay. It transpired that the former owner of the house and the land, an old man who I had never met, had signed the transfer deed to the house, but had dragged his heels over signing the one corresponding to the land. She explained that he was a very old man indeed, now living with his slightly younger sister, and it was at that time that he had begun to suffer from transitory delusions. "Qué delusiones?" I asked, hoping that the word was the same in Spanish. Delusions, she said, that he would soon be well enough to cultivate the land again. He was happy to sign over the house, as he was well looked after at his sister's, but the land was a different matter; the land had more 'pull'.

I sympathised with the longings of a fellow lover of the earth and suggested that he come round to the house to see that his beloved plot - now my beloved plot - was being well cared for. He might make suggestions for future crops and even enjoy some of the fruits of my future labours. He was welcome to spend time there and reminisce about the good old days of working in the fields from sunrise to sundown; ploughing and planting, tending and harvesting his precious crops. And while he was round one day, he could sign the transfer deed.

Miguel translated all this rapidly, the young lady nodding all the while, and they both fell silent, possibly stunned by my eloquence. The problem, Miguel finally said, was that the man was now worse. He was now suffering from severe dementia and would not be deemed fit to sign the deed even if he consented to. The young lady said that the council had sent several letters to the man's sister's house requesting his presence, and that the sister herself had recently come in to tell them that he was now like a goat. On seeing my confusion, Miguel apologised for his literal translation and said that 'like a goat' in Spanish meant insane. He then apologised again, as, when he said insane, he really meant to say demented, or rather, that the poor man was suffering from dementia.

The upshot of all this is that there is nothing to be done but wait. Miguel said that when the man dies, his sister will inherit, and, as she is as 'compos mentis' as anybody else in this town, she will sign over the land. He told me not to worry and that he had just wanted me to know the 'state of play'. Before we parted on the town hall steps, I asked Miguel how it was that I had not received an official letter about today's meeting. He said that Paula, the official, was his cousin and that she was the mayor's daughter-in law. He himself, he said, considered me a friend, so they had dispensed with that trivial formality. My friend Miguel still charged me €50 for his services.

When Paco came round for our class, I told him that I did not feel up to a Country and Western song tonight; indeed, I had the almond liqueur and two glasses already prepared. I told him in detail about today's events and he told me not to worry, as this kind of thing was perfectly normal. He then uttered his first unsung English words for a long time. He just said, "This is Spain."

Viernes, 14 de Marzo

A cloudy day full of cloudy thoughts. I certainly think the Spanish have a peculiar way of going about things. Dispensing with official letters due to family ties! It is refreshing and, at the same time, worrying; more worrying than refreshing, in fact. We shall just have to wait for the old man to pass away and then deal with his sister. She will hopefully hang on to her faculties in the meantime, as I know from my own family history that these matters are often hereditary.

I am so looking forward to our second game of golf tomorrow, now that a linguistic 'entente' has been achieved! We will both be able to concentrate on our game, though I fear Alfredo's is the stronger due to my lack of practice. I will, nevertheless, dispense with any underhand tactics this time.

One hour of golfing vocabulary on the internet. As it is a new sport here, they don't have the wealth of expressions that we have - 'drain a snake' and 'frog hair', for instance - and instead employ standard language.

Sábado, 15 de Marzo

A fine, sunny day for our fine second game! Having agreed that conversation on the drive down to the course and the first nine holes were to be conducted in Spanish, I opened proceedings by asking Alfredo what he did for a living. He is an 'abogado' (lawyer) and is a partner in what he considers to be the best law practice in Villeda. This was gratifying to know, as it is always useful to be able to count a good lawyer amongst ones friends. I told him about my recent town hall tribulations and he said that I had no need to worry. Miguel, Paula and Alberto, the mayor, were all fine, trustworthy people; something that could not be said for the public servants in some nearby towns that he could mention, who were all 'hijos de la gran puta' ('sons, and possibly daughters, of the great whore'). He went on to say that he and Alberto were members of the same Easter 'Cofradía' (fraternity) and that he was Paula's godfather.

Alfredo enjoyed the drive down to the course in the Peugeot and said that it brought back fond memories of his grandfather's car, which was the same model, but black, due to him being the town undertaker. We teed off into the sun and I found that my absorption in the game reduced my Spanish speech to a trickle. I have never been able to concentrate on two difficult tasks at the same time, such as hanging a picture and helping Gerald with his maths homework, and opted to centre my attention on the match, which was stroke play today. After holing a fine four yard putt at the ninth, I was trailing Alfredo by seven shots (54 to his 47), but was confident that the strain of speaking English would diminish his game somewhat.

I had pledged myself to employ no foul means this time, but could not resist following up each of Alfredo's rudimentary remarks with a question. This diverted his brain enough for me to claw back four shots on the back nine, and I accepted my narrow defeat gracefully. I joked that I may be fifteen years older than him, but that my greater experience and tactical skill would prevail in the end. He said that answering my constant questions had cost him at least half a dozen shots and that, if I continued to improve, he would bring earplugs. He laughed and called me a bastard again, which is nowhere near as offensive as it would be in English, Pamela tells me, unless they employ the actual word 'bastardo', which they take very literally indeed.

On reaching home and coming in to greet Pamela, Alfredo urged us to go to watch the Easter procession in Villeda the following Friday, Good Friday, as he would be taking part. We said that we would certainly attend, and he promised to nod to us so that we would recognise him. This leads me to understand that they march in some kind of fancy dress.

Lunes, 17 de Marzo

A cloudy but pleasant day. I was doing a little weeding this morning when Andy rang to say that he would bring the rotavator round on Wednesday, so I stopped weeding right away and ordered the house sign on the internet. They state that it will arrive within the week, so they certainly work quickly. Pamela called me in for a 'cuppa' and gave me a milk-less drink that tasted very strange. It was, she said, an infusion of the herbs that Angeles had given her, and had great digestive properties. While I digested it, she told me that she would very much like to create a herb garden. I pointed out that my priority was to plant that essential foodstuff which would keep our bodies and souls together and that I might not have time to plant inessential items. She replied that I had misunderstood her and that *she* was going to create the herb garden and that she had already started to read up on the subject 'online'. Where, she wanted to know, would I like her to put it? I suggested a square yard or two of land down at the end of the plot near to the track, but she said that she knew I was going to say that. "It will be here, next to the terrace, so I can get at it when I am cooking," she said, and, did I prefer it to be to the left or to the right of the door? "You choose," I said, and made myself a cup of tea to take the taste of the herbs away.

Half an hour studying herbs and spices on the internet, and half an hour marking out Pamela's small herb patch with little stones, before remembering that the rotavator would soon disperse them.

Miércoles, 19 de Marzo, 'San José' day.

A sunny day for rotavating. Andy arrived at half past nine and pushed a small package through our neighbours' letterbox. "For inspiration," he said, and asked if he should give some to the other neighbours too. I said that he most certainly should not; that Angeles needed no stimulants of any kind, and that any strange substance could push Nora over the edge. He said that he was joking, which I had half suspected, and assured me that he did not sell the stuff, which was a relief. One thing is having a 'pot head' for a friend, quite another a 'Drug Baron'. "I just share a little of a pleasurable plant that God created," he said, "the grapevine being another I could mention." He will not convince me.

He wheeled the rotavator, or 'mula mecánica', through the

house, started it up, and I set to work. It is not at all easy to direct the clumsy machine in a straight line, and I had soon inadvertently ploughed up some of the potatoes, much to Andy's delight. They were disappointingly under-developed, so I continued down the line, while Andy popped them into a bucket. "Three or four plates of chips there," he said, which was most discouraging. He said that winter potato crops were notably 'crap' and that I'd have more luck next time. He said he might as well pick the onions while he was at it, for what they were worth. They were hardly bigger than pickled onions, but he said to leave the garlic until the leaves began to shrivel and I would get something worthwhile. Just my luck that the only thing I don't like is the only thing that may be a success.

I allowed Andy to take over the ploughing for a while, as my arms were turning to jelly, and soon the plot was once again as it had been four months earlier, apart from the almost lifeless trees and the garlic. Andy said that he didn't plant much in winter as a rule, but as I had seemed so keen, he had not wanted to discourage me. 'Something ventured, nothing gained' springs to mind as a suitable adaptation of the old refrain. One lives and learns.

We chatted over a pre-lunch glass of beer and I told Andy of my disenchantment with the car. He suggested we go to see Arturo and trade it in for a sensible car, as no-one else would give me more than a pittance for it. He added that Arturo knew a lot of gypsies and that they were keen on that sort of car for taking their goods to market. "They keep their proper car for best," he said.

I will not stay up to see the San José celebration in Valencia on television, as I have already seen footage of them burning the beautifully made sculptures, which is such a waste. The

Spaniards do seem to have a destructive streak, although I suppose if they didn't burn them, they wouldn't be able to make new 'Fallas', as they are known, for next year.

Jueves, 20 de Marzo

Light rain, slowly seeping into my almost virginal plot all day. Today's class was the most dramatic so far. As I thought I knew the effect that the chosen song would have on Paco, I preferred to get our Spanish chat out of the way first. I am now able to speak quite competently with Paco, more so than with other people, and I think this is because he knows exactly what I do, and do not, understand. He throws in new words every now and again, and allows me to ramble on for a while before stopping me and pointing out my mistakes. He is becoming my made to measure Spanish mentor!

'Coat of Many Colors' is, I know, a touching song, but the effect of my arduously prepared translation on Paco was greater than even his previous mushiness had prepared me for. As the moral of the story of the patchwork coat unfolded, Paco, already sniffling, burst into tears and said that it was the most beautiful thing he had ever heard. When he had composed himself enough to sing the song, his voice gradually turned into a harrowing wail reminiscent of the Flamenco style, at which point Pamela peeped around the door to see if anything was amiss. On finishing the song alone, for I had already fallen into silence, Paco slumped forward onto the table in exhaustion. Pamela returned shortly after with a camomile infusion to restore his nervous system and told Paco that he had achieved the first known 'fusion' of Flamenco and

Country music, which ought to be recorded for posterity. Paco, however, felt too weak to repeat his performance and sat sipping his infusion until he felt ready for an almond liqueur.

Viernes, 21 de Marzo

Today is 'Viernes Santo' and not 'Buen Viernes' as I called it in the rustic bar earlier, resulting in much laughter from the assembled peasantry. This is a very late diary entry, us having just returned from seeing the processions in Villeda.

The drizzle had not abated by sunset, so we arrived early enough to find a table under the veranda of a corner café, from where to view the proceedings in relative comfort. The streets were lined with people of all ages, and we prepared ourselves for what promised to be a varied and entertaining evening, judging by the expectancy of the crowds. After about an hour we heard the sound of melancholy music, which heralded the first procession. Elegantly robed men carrying sundry crosses and flags passed first, followed by more men shouldering an effigy of a very bloodied and undernourished Christ. A large band, comprised mostly of old men and young teenagers, brought up the rear, playing their mournful music to the slow beat of a drum which seemed far bigger than the little fat boy who was bashing it. When they had all finally passed, the crowd strained to see the next contribution to the evening's entertainment, which turned out to be another group of men, a float of a flaky Virgin Mary, followed by another band. The third 'turn' of the evening surprised me by their sporting of Klu Klux Klan style hooded robes, which seemed most peculiar and a little macabre. I could not see any coloured people present, which may have been just as well. One of these hooded men appeared to have a twitch, which caused his pointed hat to quiver, until we realised that it must be Alfredo trying to subtly catch our attention. We waved at him and he released a finger from his cross and wiggled it, so we were almost sure it *was* him.

This was the high point of the evening, as all that followed was more and more of the same. By the time an extra-large Virgin was carted past, both our bottoms were sore and Pamela was tipsy. I too would have liked to have indulged a little more, in order to relieve the intense boredom, but I simply refuse to 'drink drive'. We followed the crowd to the church square, where a rendition of Ave Maria was hooted out by a troop of sweaty cornetists, before beating a retreat.

On the way home, I pointed out that the rather young-looking, second to last Virgin carried a picture of a grown up Christ, which was not historically accurate. Pamela said that a virgin birth could presumably be performed at any age, and asked me if I would be 'Klukluxklanning it' with Alfredo next year. I replied that I would certainly not be taking part in such 'pompous popery', which I thought humorously alliterative.

Sábado, 22 de Marzo

As golf was not possible yesterday, due to Alfredo's continuing Easter commitments, I put some more diesel in the guzzling brute and we headed off to the car-boot sale. I made a beeline for the book-swindler's stall and found him bedazzling a northern English couple with his pidgin sales patter. "Nice big shiny atlas looking good on coffee table," he said, and, "cheap big old books here only €20 for ten." I warned the northern gentleman of the Spaniard's crookedness and told him the tale of volume sixty-two. "Eh lad," he said, "we's only wuntin a bit er bulk on't shelves, a bit er colour, like." So perhaps northerners are every bit as uncultured as they are said to be, after all.

When they had tottered away under the weight of a dozen volumes which they will never be able to read, I turned to the rogue and said, "Y volumen sesenta y dos, qué?" He feigned ignorance, so I reminded him of my recent purchase, to which he replied with words to the effect (I thought, and Pamela later confirmed) of, 'How the hell was I supposed to know that a book was missing and who the hell cares? No-one is going to read the old pile of crap, are they?'

I said that I certainly *was* going to read; was in fact reading, the 'old pile of crap', and what kind of bookseller was he anyway? He said he was a poor one, and one that was 'hasta los cojones de los guiris de mierda' – an astonishingly vulgar way of saying, 'fed up to the back teeth of shitty foreigners'; using the equivalent of 'bollocks' instead of our more refined 'back teeth'. He told me I was like a goat and stomped off to his van and slammed the door. I shouted that *he* was like a goat, before Pamela ushered me away to see if the desk and chair were still there. Making him apoplectic gave me some satisfaction, but it will not bring back volume sixty-two.

The desk and chair were still on sale and, feeling strong after my victory, I browbeat the Moroccan down to €180 and made him and his skinny sidekick carry the desk to the car to boot (unintended and confusing pun). The Line Dancing contingent, seemingly a regular fixture at the car-boot sale, were most amused by the tale of my day's exploits, and the Welsh woman said, "That's right. Got to keep these foreigners in their place," which I thought was rich coming from a person who is a foreigner everywhere except in a clump of hills tacked onto the side of England.

The desk looks splendid in the study, and a collection of Trollope I picked up sits nicely on the shelves. I have never read Trollope, but, on recalling the northern man's comments, have determined to at least have a go at 'Barchester Towers'. Pamela says that he is very good and that he also invented the postbox, something that most modern writers cannot boast of.

Lunes, 24 de Marzo

A fine day, which makes me itch to start planting. While strolling around in my study this morning, Pamela appeared and said that she supposed that I had no further use for the table, which was now pushed back against the wall. I agreed that the table did rather lower the tone of the room, to which she said that she would like it moving into the as yet unfurnished bedroom. I remarked that it made a poor substitute for a bed, and she replied that she intended to convert the room into a classroom. I said that Paco and I needed no formal setting for our increasingly informal meetings, and she replied that she wasn't thinking about me and Paco. Enigmatic as ever, she went down to prepare lunch without another word.

Over lunch it transpired that Laura has suggested that the children of the village would benefit from some extra English tuition. I pointed out to Pamela that I was just about to embark on my spring planting and that I would be far too occupied with my horticultural tasks to think about the education of the local tearaways. She said that she thought I might say something like that, but it was she who proposed to impart the classes, once a group of half a dozen or so were established. She also said, if I recall correctly, "I'll charge them each a pittance, but if there are six of them it'll be a nice bit of extra cash. I shall need six more chairs and will find them at the car boot sale on Saturday."

Saturdays are now, for me, synonymous with golf, and I said so, to which Pamela replied, "Getting hooked again, are we? After all you said about never playing again!" She did add, much to my relief, that she was perfectly capable of driving to the sale without me and that Laura would be happy to accompany her.

The thought of the village children, possibly even the one who hit me on the nose with a snowball, tramping through my house and destroying my language is not a pleasant one, but Pamela seems set on the idea, so that, as far as that is concerned, is that. I am hopeful that none of the urchins will wish to take part, as regular school is normally quite sufficient 'book learning' for the rural youngster.

Half an hour of 'This Ole House', an upbeat song which will hopefully give Paco's tear ducts a rest, and half an hour of 'The Grapes of Wrath', which is hard going due to the translator's insistence on trying to replicate the Judd family's bumpkin speech.

Miércoles, 26 de Marzo

This morning we drove coastward to the impressive 'viverista' in Andy's van. Everything we need seems to lie towards the coast. Following Andy's expert guidance, I bought trays of pepper, tomato, lettuce, aubergine, leek and celery plants, as well as a pair each of young almond and olive trees, and a multitude of assorted seeds, which Andy insisted would not 'go off' as I had feared. Pamela and I can make another trip to pick up her trifling herbs, unless she prefers to come with Laura or another of her friends, now that she is asserting her independence as never before.

On our return and after a quick lunch, I threw myself into a frenzy of planting, following Andy's instructions on depth, distancing and the like. By six o'clock, all my purchases were in the ground and I finished watering them an hour ago. I am happy, exhausted, and ever so grateful for my friend's help and advice. If we ever go back to Britain, I would very much like to make a tour of Scotland, which I have never visited, as its people have risen considerably in my estimations, something I cannot yet say for the Welsh.

Pamela has bought a white blackboard, an easel, an eraser, marker pens, pens, grammar books, exercise books, a box of white card, and some Harry Potter hats. At this rate it will take her some time to begin to profit from the as yet hypothetical classes.

Viernes, 28 de Marzo

In yesterday's class, Paco returned to a state of relative composure, as 'This Ole House' could evoke no soppiness regarding past abodes; he was born in the house in which he lives.

The plot is looking glorious in today's sunshine. I trust that if or when Gerald comes to visit, he will be suitably impressed by my horticultural, or 'ecological', labours. I foresee no need to tell him that I did not grow everything from the seed. I planted potatoes, onions, peas, carrots and parsley today, so my initial labours are complete. Now all that remains is to keep everything watered, weeded and in trim. Andy says that the plot should need no fertilizer or manure this year, as it has lain fallow for a long time, and that he will provide me with any pesticides which he considers absolutely necessary, if any. Paco, of course, would have me douse the lot with every poison under the sun. His 'modern' farming methods are all very well for filling the supermarket shelves, but we shan't be using such tainted produce for much longer anyway.

Pamela's little herb plot, newly demarcated with stones, lies barren while she spends her time writing words on her pieces of card. These, she says, are called 'flashcards' and will form the backbone of her teaching method, something she has been researching avidly on the internet. I hope she will not be disappointed, but suspect that few of the little savages will sign up.

Half an hour reading about modern teaching methods, and half an hour practising my golf swing.

Domingo, 30 de Marzo

Yesterday's game of golf was a little frustrating, to say the least. On my third outing I expected my game to improve a little, but it did not. Added to this, Alfredo decided to employ my tactic of continually questioning me during today's Spanish speaking back nine. This was very unfair, as I had spoken very little during the first nine holes, enabling him to build up a lead of six shots (46 to my 52). He finally beat me by a dozen shots and, as we put away our putters, said that he had no further questions, before doubling over with laughter. He said, "Te he jodido hoy, eh?" which I later found to mean, 'I have f**cked you today, eh?', which Pamela says, as always, is not as vulgar in Spanish as in English, but, in this case, is not far off. We have agreed that, from now on, no questions, baffling phrases or impertinent comments are to be permitted during the game itself.

While I was golfing, Pamela visited the car boot sale with Laura and picked up six folding chairs for €50, having haggled so pitilessly with a big, bald German that he tracked her down to the makeshift café to accept her meagre offer. She drove a hard bargain, I must admit, but it still adds to her capital outlay on the yet to commence classes.

Today the sun has shone kindly on my plot, which I enjoyed watering this morning. When Pamela came out with a cup of tea, I was watering her little plot, sighing pointedly as I did so. She said I was not to worry, as she would soon be sprinkling some seeds there. She will soon find out that horticulture is much more complicated than merely 'sprinkling seeds'!

The Judd family in 'The Grapes of Wrath' is not a happy one. Their lamentations regarding the homestead that they over-exploited and lost are very touching, especially to a fellow landowner like myself. Now in sunny California, they pick the crops of others to feed the 'capitalist beast'. I shall ask Gerald if he has read the book when he comes.

A new month and one of great promise! The winter has long gone, although it was not as short as I was led to believe, and we have the whole summer to look forward to. Pamela has made no further mention of central heating and I hope that the warm weather will put it out of her mind until it is too late to do anything about it. Pamela wishes our next trip to be to Madrid and says that we will go by train. This reminds me of a travel book I once read by a man with a French name, in which he travelled to Japan and back solely on trains. He said that this was the way for a true traveller to meet and talk to people, and he certainly seemed to have a jolly time. If our future travels are to be by train, I may as well keep the old Peugeot for now, as my runs into town will hardly break the bank as much as buying a newer car would. No new car, no central heating, and an impending abundance of home grown vegetables; this will be a balm to our bank account!

Pamela has just announced that her first class will take place on Thursday evening at about the same time as my 'class' with Paco. She is not sure exactly how many children will turn up and says that she will improvise according to numbers. She showed me the 'flashcards' she has made, including colours, simple adjectives and my old favourite, the verb 'to be'. She practised on me with the adjectives and I knew them all, although she says that I still pronounce the single 'r' too weakly and the double 'r' like a machine gun. We will see if she is such a 'clever clogs' if nobody comes to her class.

Jueves, 3 de Abril

A quiet day, followed by a most perturbing evening. Just as Paco and I were settling down in my study to work on 'Behind Closed Doors', we felt that we weren't in fact behind closed doors at all, as a cacophony of yelping children thundered up the stairs and into the spare bedroom/classroom. The level of noise descended perceptibly when Pamela's voice was also heard and then picked up again as they began chanting, "gren, yeyo, braun, bluey," much to my amusement. Soon, however, this changed to, "green, yellow, brown, blue," and was followed by some acceptably pronounced numbers, some basic 'to be' phrases, and a smattering of 'I like (various things)'. After listening for a while, I remembered that Paco was present, waiting to learn his song. We sang very quietly today, through fear of being heard by the youngsters, and agreed that we may have to change our night. When I heard the scraping of chairs, I opened the study door slightly and was able to observe NINE contented-looking children between the approximate ages of seven and twelve descending the stairs in an almost orderly fashion.

Pamela then joined us for a glass of almond liqueur, flushed with satisfaction at the success of her first class. We congratulated her and I proposed a toast to her new venture, "To the civilisation of the barbarians," which Paco understood and seconded. He regretted that his seventeen year old son, also called Paco, was too old to join the class, as he had been studying English for ten years at school and appeared to know less than those little ones had learnt in an hour. Pamela said that she was happy to organise a more advanced class for the teenagers, which pleased Paco and pleased me rather less. Tonight is not the time to clip Pamela's wings, however, as she deserves to bask awhile in her unexpected success.

Viernes, 4 de Abril

My pleasure on receiving the wooden house name - which is very well made, despite having come straight from China after having been ordered from Britain - was soon tempered by a double bombshell from Pamela. The first bombshell came in the shape of a man in blue overalls, who arrived to give us a quote for a central heating system. I should have expected this after the initial firmness of Pamela's words on the subject, and should also have expected the second bombshell, which was that she did indeed intend to organise another English group for teenagers, and may even consider yet *another* one for adults. "I am only fifty-two," she said, "and have always worked at least part-time. I don't intend to retire just yet." I suppose she is right, and she doesn't have the great responsibility of an agricultural plot on her shoulders as I do. I only hope that Pamela's pursuit of increased self-esteem does not prevent me from relaxing after a hard day of working the land.

I put up the house name to the left of the front door. It looks as refined as it does rustic, and I only hope that a sign saying 'Pamela's School of English for Country Folk' does not appear by its side.

Domingo, 6 de Abril

Yesterday's golf commenced under heavy clouds, quite reminiscent of many of my games in England, and a cloudburst after the eleventh dampened Alfredo's body and spirits considerably; he having failed to stow the all-important waterproof in his golf trolley, unlike myself. His game fell to pieces, while mine stayed much the same, and I ate into his seven shot lead. Teeing off at the last hole we were even, and my fine, if not over-long, drive put victory within reach. We both reached the green in three and, as I squared up for a long putt, Alfredo asked me if I knew how much the central heating was going to cost. Up until then we had adhered to our agreement of only speaking between holes and never asking thought-provoking questions. I answered that I didn't know, but the digits that inevitably began to whirr inside my brain caused me to skew the putt to the left, leaving the ball five yards from the hole. He holed in five to my seven and I was thoroughly annoyed and quite unable to speak until I had drunk a glass of beer and Alfredo had ordered me a second. He apologised for his misdemeanour and said that if he had known I was going to take it so badly, he would never have asked the question, but that he did feel that I had used this tactical distraction much more than him in our previous games. I said that it was only a game and made an attempt to be civil on the drive home, but the Spaniards' reputation for being cruel and devious may hold some truth after all.

Yesterday's rain and today's sun have made the plot come to life before my eyes! Even the trees are showing signs of growth, and I had a most enjoyable weeding session, before taking Pamela a cup of tea and finding her amidst a sea of 'flashcards'. She tells me that she has ordered some suitable posters for the walls, so the spare bedroom does in fact seem destined to be a classroom. I suggested that I might be able to share some of her teaching responsibilities and she asked me if I required her assistance on the plot. I said that I didn't and she said, "Well, then?" I took this to be a negative and asked if she still intended to plant her herbs, as I could well use the three square yards for something else. "All in good time," she replied, and returned to her regular verbs.

Half an hour of irregular verbs and half an hour looking through Pamela's 'flashcards' to make sure I knew them all. I did, much to my relief.

Martes, 8 de Abril

I went for a brisk walk yesterday morning, something I must remember to do more regularly, and, on my return, Pamela stated that she had finished sowing her herbs. I went to look and, apart from some slight movement of the soil, I could see no sign of horticultural activity or organisation; no boundaries, no little signs to mark each herb, nothing. A few seeds were actually visible, and I wouldn't be surprised if she hadn't just sprinkled a mixed bag on the patch and rushed back to her classroom. She is probably right in that we should each concentrate on our own projects, as I don't think that horticulture (or, 'herbiculture?') is her strong point. She says I may water her little patch when I water the main plot, so it appears that she considers her work done.

Pamela told her Line Dancing friends about her classes, which, she claims, generated some interest. It appears that even those confirmed expats, clinging as they do to their foreign dancing traditions, know quite a few Spanish people and have promised to spread the word. The Welsh woman says that her neighbours in the country, a middle-aged couple, once asked *her* about English classes for themselves, and that she would let them know about Pamela's services. I quipped that she could perhaps introduce the Welsh language into the valley of Villeda, and Pamela said that she - and she reminded me that she has a name: Nerys - does not, in fact, speak Welsh. How, then, did she get that frightfully Welsh accent?

Pamela hogged the computer all afternoon, printing out leaflets to advertise her classes. I feel a little left out of all this activity - there is only so much one can do on the plot at this time of year - and may renew my offer of assistance. I have more experience of teaching adults, namely Paco, than Pamela, and the 'flashcards' would enable one to always stay one step ahead of the students. I shall not, however, plead.

Jueves, 10 de Abril

During my walk in the country this warm, sunny morning, on passing 'Casa Harrison' I beheld a sight, an eyesore in fact, that made me shudder. A couple a little older than Pamela and myself, presumably the Harrisons, were sunning their almost naked bodies within full view of the track. She was 'topless' and her breasts floundered against her stout body in a most disagreeable way; I am sure you could incubate an ostrich's egg under each of them. (Excessively vulgar: edit from published diary, or at least check on size of ostrich eggs.) He had a book propped open on his huge stomach, but appeared to be nodding off - at half past eleven in the morning!

This then, is the life of the typical expat from now until the autumn. Mindlessly and uselessly - for it will do little to increase their beauty - they will laze about from morning till night, soaking up the sun's rays, heedless of the impression they create on the native population and the damage they do to the reputation of industrious and 'integrationist' newcomers such as Pamela and myself. I will continue to wear long trousers for as long as I can bear it.

Paco and I had not changed our day for the class, as I wished to hear what Pamela was teaching next door without being forced to eavesdrop; so, once the mob had settled, we settled down to a variation on our regular syllabus. Instead of the 'Sunday Morning Coming Down' that Paco had expected me to have translated for him, he found himself face to face with a set of food and drink 'flashcards'. I told him that I had not had the time to translate yet another Country and Western song; that, indeed, we were fast running out of 'standards', and that, in view of the craze for English that appeared to be about to take the village by a storm, it was time we knuckled down once again.

I told Paco that it was, in principle, only for today, and proceeded to work through the cards, eliciting the correct pronunciation through much repetition. After twenty minutes, he knew each item off by heart and we spent the final ten minutes liking fish, disliking milk and so forth. Paco's grand finale was, "I like beef, I like lettuce, and I like Country and Western music very, very, very much!" In our Spanish half hour I told him that I was prepared to forsake my Spanish half hour in favour of half an hour of English followed by a Country and Western song. There would be time enough for Spanish chatter over the almond liqueur. I did, however, say, "No English, no Country and Western song," to which Paco replied, "No woman, no cry," which is a good, if rather irrelevant, sign.

Pamela said that her class went very well and that she needed to procure more folding chairs, as eleven students had presented themselves today. I told her about my qualified success with Paco and she congratulated me. I said that I thought I was rather good with adult students and she said, "We will see," without elaborating on what we might see. A ray of hope, at least.

Sábado, 12 de Abril

Alfredo called me last night to say that he could not play golf today, due to having to attend an urgent work-related meeting in Madrid. Remembering his unsportsmanlike behaviour last week, I expressed little regret, although I felt it, and we agreed to meet next Saturday as usual. Golfless, I sat on the terrace and ruminated on the plot, when it suddenly occurred to me that it should not just be me ruminating, but other beasts too! Of course! Man cannot, normally, live on vegetables alone, and so obsessed was I with the plot that I hadn't even considered getting any living, breathing, livestock! I rushed up to the classroom to share my brainwave with Pamela and she said that she had feared that this moment would come. She had, she said, begged Andy not to encourage me to keep any animals, as they were such smelly, noisy creatures, but did suppose that I would eventually come up with the idea myself.

Well, I had, I said, and any self-respecting liver-off-the-land had to have *some* animals. I rushed off to the computer, rapidly typed in 'animals for plots', and received information regarding dramatic plots involving household pets, wild animals plotting to attack humans, and suchlike. I then tried 'animals for your smallholding' and met with more success. One article suggested starting off with small animals such as chickens and rabbits, before moving on to turkeys, pigs, goats, sheep, alpacas and ostriches. I discounted the final two, for now, and decided to mentally work through the rest in reverse order. I have never seen a sheep in Spain, so it might be too warm for them in summer, although I have eaten some tasty lamb chops, possibly imported. As for pigs, I shall have to see Andy's father-in-law slaughter one before I will know if I have the stomach to do so myself. Also, as far as I know, they produce no milk fit for human consumption. Goats are friendly-looking creatures, but could they be trained to only eat the weeds and not the vegetables on the plot? I doubt it. Turkeys are ugly, mean-looking birds which are only considered edible once a year. Rabbits? I believe they are generally kept as pets, although some Spanish recipes contain pieces of them. Chickens it is, then.

"Chickens, then, to start with," I said to Pamela, to which she replied that I had at least eliminated the less practical ones without her help. She supposed that, "a little coop down by the track, *away* from the house," would at least keep us in eggs, and that it wouldn't be strictly necessary to butcher any of them. She then added, and I reproduce her exact words, "So you are in favour of animals, in principle, then?" "Yes," I replied. "Good," she said, and went back to her class preparation. In view of what I had already told her, it was an oddly timed question, which leads me to believe that she is plotting something.

One hour reading up on chicken breeding. I shall need at least one cock, or all will be in vain.

Lunes, 14 de Abril

I spent most of yesterday studying chicken coop architecture, finally concluding that those apparently simple structures are quite complex in nature and that it would be far easier to buy one online. I ordered a flat-pack 'gallinero' bearing the very un-Spanish name of 'Little Farm' from a Spanish supplier, and eagerly await its arrival. I drove out to Andy's house this morning and 'picked his brains' about poultry matters. They are, he says, very low-maintenance creatures and he will supply me with two layers, four promising young chickens and his number three cock, which, he said, "gets laid less than me right now." He will only accept a very small amount of money for these birds, and that after much insistence.

Impending motherhood has made Ana more beautiful than ever, and she told me that there has been much interest in Pamela's advertisement for classes which she put up at her school. I told her that I may well be assisting with the adult classes, to which she just replied, "Ah," and smiled. I think she is dubious of my teaching ability, but perhaps she is unaware of the instant wisdom-bestowing properties of 'flashcards'!

One hour writing my own 'flashcards', to be tested on my guinea pig, Paco, and half an hour researching guinea pigs as a possible addition to my fledgling farm, before rejecting them on the grounds of their being entirely unproductive rodents.

Miércoles, 16 de Abril

Just recently bombshells have been falling about me like golf balls on a driving range. Pamela returned from Line Dancing yesterday with the unwelcome news that the Welsh woman has recently produced a litter of cocker spaniels and has offered her one. Pamela's poor wording of this news, coupled with my feeling of deflation, allowed an unusually crude remark to pass my lips, which I immediately withdrew and will not reproduce here. I am not especially fond of dogs and nor are the Spanish, unless they serve some useful purpose such as hunting things or guarding property. A pet dog is a very English, and apparently Welsh, accessory for which the productive smallholder has no use. I suspect that most expats have pet dogs too, to give themselves something to look at during their aimless, unproductive days.

I told Pamela this and she said that perhaps I was right and that our house should remain a *totally* animal-free zone, "and that would include birds," she added. I remonstrated that a dog was not productive, and she replied that it would warn against burglars, and chicken rustlers. I conceded that this was a valid point and Pamela forced home her advantage by saying that the puppies were of the 'Working Cocker' breed, and not just common or garden cocker spaniels. "It will be able to help you on the plot," she said, before going up to her classroom and closing the door. I fear that another of Pamela's 'faits accomplis' is about to be accomplished.

On a lighter note, I bumped into Miguel, our interpreter, in town this morning and he told me that the old man who still technically owns my plot appears to be on his deathbed. (Review that sentence before publication.) This is good, and at the same time sad, news, as, on his demise, his still lucid sister will finally sign over my land to me.

One hour researching 'Working Cockers' on the internet. I read that, unlike normal cockers, 'they must have a job to do', but heaven knows what tasks it will be able to perform, unless it grows fingers to pull up weeds with.

Viernes, 17 de Abril

Our tandem of English classes went very well yesterday. Through entertaining mime worthy of Nora, I taught Paco, 'I am cooking, I am dancing, I am sleeping' etc. before tackling the song. I cannot understand why Paco struggles so much to pronounce correctly the sentences he understands, while singing 'Sunday Morning Coming Down', which he understands only partially, beautifully. Next week I will sing him some new sentences and perhaps thereby invent a new teaching method! All Pamela's students came back for more and, towards the end of the class, I popped my head around the door to introduce myself. I said, "Hello, I am Ernest. How are you all?" and all answered correctly, with the exception of one small girl who burst into tears and slid under the table. I crouched down to wave to her and her shrieking was of such intensity that Pamela quickly ushered me out of the room. Adult classes, possibly 'singing classes', will be my speciality.

This morning, Pamela's new puppy came to visit. It is very small, black, clumsy and useless-looking. Nerys, for I have been told that I must use the Welsh woman's name, came round with it before lunch and gave us instructions regarding its future nutritional requirements. Alas, it could not stay, as it cannot yet tear itself away from its mother's bosom. Nerys brought it round, she said, "to get a feel for the place." I asked her if she would like me to give it a tour of the house, and Nerys, failing to understand English irony, said that it wouldn't be necessary. I said that I was all for the dog sleeping outside in a kennel, the better to guard the poultry, and they said I was cruel, heartless and barbaric. It will *not* be sleeping on my bed.

On the news today it was announced that the Spanish government is to pump ten billion Euros into the economy to 'reactivate it'. I wasn't aware that it needed reactivating, but it must, and I ask myself where they will get the ten billion from. Perhaps they still have a stash of silver and gold from their ransacking of South America.

Domingo, 20 de Abril

In yesterday's golf match I ran Alfredo closer than ever before - only one shot in it! We respected each other's languages around the course, and my putting was as good as it has been since my glory days of the early nineties, when I won the club handicap championship twice. I later asked him about the state of the Spanish economy and he gave me a 'thumbs down' sign. The whole economy, he explained with words and gestures, was centred on the housing market, and the housing market was a speculative bubble already leaking (hissing noise) and about to burst (bang!). This is not good news at all, as our house, while being a bargain, was also rather expensive.

We will never sell 'Integración', but, all the same, I would prefer it not to go down in price after all the work I am doing to *increase* its value. Perhaps Alfredo is over-dramatising, as Spaniards are wont to do.

I returned home to be met by the sight of a dog basket in the kitchen, thus confirming that the decision is final, but allaying my fears that it would be sleeping in my bedroom. I asked Pamela if the dog was going to be her responsibility, as it had been her idea, and she said that it was, although I might as well take it on my country rambles as I was going anyway. The thin end of a new wedge, I fear, though it must be said that the subject of satellite television has not yet reared its ugly, dish-shaped, head.

Today has been the hottest day of the year so far; 24° centigrade in the shade! Rather than lounging in the sun like a beached walrus, I weeded the plot and levelled the area where the chicken coop will stand. After half an hour, my trousers were sticking to my legs with sweat and I had to resort to my shorts. In the privacy of my own plot I will allow myself this luxury, but when I later went to the rustic bar for coffee, my legs were as clothed as those of the village men; the *other* village men, I should say. Until I see a pair of naked, male adult legs on the village streets, they shall not see mine.

Martes, 22 de Abril

This morning I picked up the phone only to hear Gerald's voice on the end of it, calling from Spain! I had not actually spoken to him for many months, thanks to the wonders of the internet, and I did detect a hint of an Australian accent, which I trust is reversible. He arrived in Madrid yesterday and is now visiting a 'commune' in Almería before coming here. He is teaching them, he says, how to make the best use of the available water, and added, almost as an afterthought, that they also plan to sabotage the local golf course before the end of the week. I urged him to take no part in this revolutionary activity, as his mother was very keen to see him here, rather than in prison. He replied that, as it was his idea, he felt obliged to take part. He added that it was only a 'symbolic sabotage' - a few cans of motor oil on the greens - but would let the 'capitalist earth destroyers' know that they meant business. I did not want to argue with him about this before seeing him in the flesh, and told him to call us from whichever station he wished us to pick him up from, by which I meant train or bus station.

I have mixed feelings about the sabotaging of golf courses. Almería is, of course, far too dry an area to spare water for such a decadent and unproductive use, but the golfer in me wept a little at the thought of reaching the green in three, only to encounter an oil slick between the ball and the flag. A chip shot could be the solution, and the divot that it might produce would be negligible compared to the oil damage, but I rather hope that Gerald changes his mind. A brick (with a note?) thrown through the clubhouse window would be equally symbolic, and would not disrupt anyone's game.

When Pamela returned from town with a dog blanket, a collar and lead, some doggy toys, and three bags of dog food, I told her the happy news of Gerald's imminent arrival, omitting to mention the criminal component of his week's activities. She immediately went to prepare his room, while I looked up information on prison conditions, sentences for sabotage and criminal damage, bail terms and suchlike on the Spanish internet, without much success.

Jueves, 24 de Abril

The spare room now awaits Gerald's arrival, and Pamela is rarely more than ten yards away from the telephone. She said that I did not seem very thrilled about his visit and I strongly denied this. "I am on tenterhooks," I told her, and I most certainly am. At the time of writing, he may be languishing in a cell with common criminals, arguing over which television channel to watch.

I rang Miguel, the interpreter, who has no further news regarding the health of the former plot owner. He told me not to worry, as he would soon be dead, almost totally misinterpreting the reason for my call. He says that he will keep me posted, as the old man and his sister are his wife's parents' uncles, once removed. Sometimes I think all Spanish people are related. He added that, "The bucket will be surely kicked in the coming week or so," which is an odd, if not quite erroneous, use of English.

The heat continues and I spent an hour watering the plot this evening. It is a soothing activity and helped to take my mind off Gerald's impending incarceration and Pamela's reaction to it, which I fear most of all.

Sábado, 26 de Abril

After today's round (Alfredo, 88; Ernest, 97), I asked Alfredo if golf courses were often sabotaged in Spain. "No, why should they be?" he said, and wondered who on earth would wish to do such a thing. I said that 'ecologists' and 'environmentalists' might wish to do such a thing and he laughed and said that they were too few and too stupid to organise anything. I taught him, through words and gestures, the expression, 'couldn't organise a piss up in a brewery', which he found very funny. I hoped that Gerald had remembered to organise the escape route element of the sabotage. I shall be having strong words with him if he arrives.

The leaves of the garlic plants are turning brown! This means that they will soon shrivel and be ready to harvest. I shall wait for Gerald's arrival before digging them up. I hope there will be a decent crop, although I still have no desire to eat them myself. Pamela says that Gerald may well have some tips for me regarding the plot, as he too is engaged in agricultural activity, and I said that I would listen to any sensible suggestions. I may have to keep him away from the rustic bar, as the bullfighting season has commenced and they are very fond of watching it on television there. I have mixed feelings about bullfighting, but am sure that Gerald will be against it and will tell everybody so, tarring me with the brush of foreign intolerance in the process.

I think I shall have to attend a bullfight in order to decide if it is as barbaric as it looks on television. Paco says that the bulls are bred solely for this purpose and that they have a very enjoyable life until the day of the 'corrida'. So, is it better to suffer at the end, rather than never to have existed? I am not a philosopher, so I cannot say, but the bullfighters look very noble and serious and say that the bulls are their friends. Paco is my friend, but I have no desire to skewer him in the neck, except when he continually mispronounces the same words. I must remember to try out my 'Singing English' (©?) teaching method on him.

No news from Gerald. It is six days since I spoke to him, and I am beginning to worry, which is not like me. Pamela is pacing around like a prisoner in her cell, little knowing that her son may be doing the same in a real one. Looking on the bright side, if he has been arrested, he would surely have been allowed to call us. I was about to expound this theory, but stopped myself just in time. I said that he was probably hitch-hiking towards us as we spoke, which made Pamela fear that he may have been murdered en route. To take her mind off Gerald, I asked her when the puppy would be taking up residence, and she said, "bugger the puppy," which indicates that her stress levels are rising to dangerous heights.

Reasoning that he may, in fact, arrive at any moment, I weeded the plot with unusual fervour, leaving not a single unscheduled stalk standing, before watering yet again. I hope it rains soon, or our water bill will be sky high.

Miércoles, 30 Abril

Our first six months at 'Integración' have ended joyously! Gerald has called to say he will reach Villeda tomorrow, and the old man has died. I mean by this that the old man's suffering is now over, if he was suffering, and that his sister, after a respectful delay for grieving purposes, will be asked to sign the land over to its rightful owner - me. Pamela took

Gerald's call, so I don't know if he has escaped the clutches of the law since I spoke to him. She said that he said that he had had a most entertaining time on the commune, so I suspect that the sabotage went ahead. I will be grilling him on this matter, after a respectful delay for welcoming purposes.

The first half-year has flown by and I feel that things are going to plan, if not in exactly the way I foresaw them. Our budding teaching careers, for example, are a wholly unexpected development and one which I relish. It will bring us into contact with many local people and set us apart from the expat droves. My farming - for it will no longer be mere horticulture once the chickens arrive - is set to go from strength to strength, and I do not discount the possibility of requiring more land in the near future. Perhaps our talented neighbours will lease me their scrapyard, minus the cars, for my expansion.

Pamela has made today's joy slightly less complete by pointing out that we will have several visitors from England in the coming months and, what is worse, will be going there ourselves to visit her beloved but ageing aunt and other minor relatives. I protested that a farmer cannot absent himself from his farm, but she pointed out that Andy, Paco, and even Nora, would be happy to pop in to water the plants and to feed the chickens. She is yet to understand the complexities of agricultural life.

As I closed my journal, something struck me, so I opened it again to write this. Gerald must not find out that I am playing golf, or all my horticultural, cultural and linguistic progress will have been, from his extremist point of view, in vain. I must speak to Pamela about the need for secrecy regarding this matter right away.

To be continued…

arlowe.barrybraithwaite@gmail.com

CPSIA information can be obtained at www.ICGtesting.com
Printed in the USA
LVOW07s1840080315

429668LV00027B/810/P